3/17

GONE

ALSO BY
LISA McMANN

Wake

Fade

GONE

The final book in the Wake trilogy

LISA McMANN

SIMON PULSE

NEW YORK   LONDON   TORONTO   SYDNEY

SIMON PULSE

An imprint of Simon & Schuster Children's Publishing Division
1230 Avenue of the Americas, New York, NY 10020
First Simon Pulse hardcover edition February 2010
Copyright © 2010 by Lisa McMann
For information about special discounts for bulk purchases, please contact Simon & Schuster
Special Sales at 1-866-506-1949 or business@simonandschuster.com.
The Simon & Schuster Speakers Bureau can bring authors to your live event. For more
information or to book an event contact the Simon & Schuster Speakers Bureau
at 1-866-248-3049 or visit our website at www.simonspeakers.com.
Designed by Mike Rosamilia
The text of this book was set in Janson Text.
Manufactured in the United States of America
2 4 6 8 10 9 7 5 3
Library of Congress Cataloging-in-Publication Data
McMann, Lisa.
Gone / by Lisa McMann.
p. cm.
Summary: While eighteen-year-old Janie ponders her future with Cabe,
knowing that her being a dream catcher means eventual blindness and
crippling, she encounters her past as the father she never knew is
hospitalized with brain trauma and seems to need her help.
ISBN 978-1-4169-7918-0 (hardcover)
[1. Dreams—Fiction. 2. Lucid dreams—Fiction. 3. Choice—Fiction.
4. Love—Fiction. 5. Fathers and daughters—Fiction.
6. Alcoholism—Fiction.] I. Title.
PZ7.M2256Gon 2010
[Fic]—dc22
2009018682

For all those who have trouble at home.
You are not alone.

ACKNOWLEDGMENTS

Many thanks to all my invisible friends who shared their painful stories about what it's like to live with an alcoholic parent, and to Carl Loerwald at the Washtenaw Alano Club in Ann Arbor, Michigan, for all his help.

Thanks also to:

Jennifer Klonsky, whose tough suggestions made ~~me cry~~ *Gone* so much better. And, of course, to my agent, Michael Bourret, my favorite person on earth, for everything and more.

Diane Blake Harper, for being wonderful and for having the tackiest snow-globe collection ever. To Marcia and Dan Levy for all the early help—it was an honor to learn things from you. And to Joanne Levy for the priceless feedback. Go, NDP!

Matt and Kilian, for being awesome guys; Rachel Heitkamp and Kennedy, for letting me use their cool buzzword; and to Trevor Bowler, because I promised.

And to all the fans of the Wake trilogy: Thank you from the bottom of my heart for spreading the word about Janie and Cabe. You are amazing. I am grateful.

To anyone whose life is impacted by someone else's drinking problem, please check out Alateen or Al-Anon at www.al-anon.alateen.org.

JUNE 2006

24/7/365

It's like she can't breathe anymore, no matter what she does.

Like everything is closing in on her, crowding her. Threatening her.

The hearing. The truth coming out. Reliving Durbin's party in front of a judge and the three bastards themselves, staring her down. Cameras following her around the second she steps outside the courtroom. Exposed as a narc, all of Fieldridge talking about it.

Talking about her.

For weeks, it's on the local news. Gossip in the grocery store. Downtown. People point, murmur with heads close together, those looks on their faces. Randomly coming up to her and asking invasive questions. Strangers, former classmates, leaning into her space, whispering, like they're her closest confidantes: *So, what did they really do to you?*

Janie's not cut out for this—she's a loner. She is underground. It's like she hasn't even had time to let all the other stuff sink in—the real, the important. The Janie life-changing stuff. The stuff from the green notebook.

Going blind. Losing the use of her hands.

The pressure is breathtaking.
She's suffocating.
Just wants to run.
Hide.
So she can just be.

JULY 2006

Five minutes that matter.

Across the desk. The spot beside her, empty.

"I don't know anymore," she says. "I just don't know." Presses her palms into her temples, hoping her head doesn't explode.

"Whatever you decide," the woman says.

It is their secret.

AND THEN

Tuesday, August 1, 2006, 7:25 a.m.

"I can't breathe," she whispers.

His hot fingers lace her ribs, sear through her skin to her frozen lungs. He holds her. Kisses her. Breathes for her. Through her.

Makes her forget.

Afterward, he says, "We're going. Right now. Come."

She does it.

On the three-hour drive, she looks through eyelashes at her blurred fingers, curled in her lap. Pretends to be

asleep. Not sure why. Just soaking in the quiet. And knowing, deep down.

Knowing that he,

and this,

are not answers to her problems.

She's beginning to realize what is.

THE FIRST THURSDAY

August 3, 2006, 1:15 a.m.

The inquisitors are nowhere to be found on this side of the state. Here, at Charlie and Megan's rental cabin on Fremont Lake, no one knows her. The days are peaceful but the nights . . . in a tiny cabin, the nights are bad. Dreams don't take vacations when people do.

It's always something, isn't it? Always something and never nothing for Janie. Never, ever nothing.

Like the car a doctor once told her never to drive, she craves it. Craves the rebellious never, the elusive nothing. And when the next nightmare begins, she thinks about it for real.

1:23 a.m.

Janie shakes on a lumpy sofa. Beside her, stretched out in a reclining lawn chair, is Cabe. Asleep.

He's dreaming about her.

Janie watches, as she sometimes does when his dreams are sweet. Storing up memories. For later. But this . . .

They're playing paintball in an outdoor field with a dozen faceless people. It looks like a video game. Cabe and Janie move through the obstacles and shoot at each other, laughing, ducking, hiding. Cabel sneaks up and takes two shots at Janie, two red paintballs.

They nail her right in the eyeballs.

Red paint drips down her cheeks, her eye sockets hollow.

He keeps shooting and takes out one limb at a time, until Janie is just a body and a paint-striped face.

He sobs, remorseful, kneels next to her on the ground, and then picks her up and carries her, puts her in a wheelchair. Rolls her away to an empty part of the field and dumps her out onto the yellow grass.

Janie pulls out of it. Knows she shouldn't be wasting dreams. But she can't help it. She can't look away.

When she can see, she stares in the dark at the ceiling while Cabe tosses and turns. She slides her arm over her eyes, trying to forget. Trying to pretend like this hasn't been happening for two months straight, on top of everything else. "Please stop," she whispers. "Please."

4:23 a.m.

He dreams and she is forced awake again.

She holds her head.

Janie and Cabel are in the backyard of Cabe's house, sitting in the green grass. Janie's arms end at the elbows. Her eyes are sewn shut, needles still connected and hanging from the thread, down her cheeks. Black tears.

Cabel is frantic. He pulls an ear of corn from a paper grocery bag and strips the silk away. Attaches it to one of Janie's elbows. He plucks two marbles from the paper bag. Big brown Tiger's Eye shooters. He pushes them into Janie's sewn-up eyelids, pushes hard, but they won't stick. Janie falls over backward like a rag doll, unable to catch herself without hands. The ear of corn breaks off her elbow and rolls away. Cabe cradles the Tiger's Eye marbles in his hands.

Janie, numb, can't watch anymore. And she won't try to change it. Not a dream like that. Because it's about her, and how Cabe is dealing with things. It feels completely wrong to manipulate that. She just hopes he never asks her to help.

Still, she doesn't want him dreaming it, period. Not any of it. She kicks out her leg. Connects. Everything goes black.

"Sorry," he mumbles. Goes back to sleep.

It's been like this.

It's like everything he can't say comes out in his dreams.

9:20 a.m.

Familiar stirrings put an end to dreams. A welcome relief. Janie rests on her couch half-asleep. Talking herself back up. Back to normalcy. She puts on her facade.

Until she can figure out what to do about it.

About life.

About him.

9:33 a.m.

She hears the lawn chair creak, and then feels Cabel snuggling up behind her on the sofa. She stiffens, just a little. Just for a second. Then takes a deep breath. He slips his warm fingers under her cami and slides them across her belly. She smiles and relaxes, eyes still closed. "You're going to get us in trouble," she says. "You know your brother's rules."

"I'm on top of the blanket. You're under it. They'll

be okay with that. Besides, I'm not doing anything." He strokes her skin, kisses her shoulder. Slips his fingers under the waistband of her jammie pants.

"Dude." Janie links her fingers in his. "Nope," she calls out, in case Charlie and Megan are paying attention. "Nothing happening over here." She murmurs to Cabel, "You're making breakfast. Right?"

"Right. I'm starting the fire with my mind, frying bacon with my darkest, crispiest thoughts. And you thought you had a special ability. Think again, missypants."

Janie laughs, but it comes out strained. "Did you sleep okay?"

"Yeah." His chin scratches her shoulder. "Well, as good as anybody can sleep on weaved strips of fibrous plastic and a metal rod riding his ass." He nips her earlobe and adds, "Why? Did I have a nightmare? You always make me nervous when you ask that."

"Shh," Janie says. "Go make me some bacon."

He's quiet for a moment, and then he gets up. Slips into his jeans. "Okay, then."

9:58 a.m.

They do vacationy things. Sitting around with Charlie and Megan, drinking coffee, making breakfast over the campfire. Relaxing. Getting to know one another better.

Janie's distracted.

She stares at everything, afraid she'll miss something that needs to be seen before it's too late.

She really doesn't know how to do vacations.

Besides, some stuff you just can't get away from.

But she's brave. Everything appears normal. Even though inside, she's wrecked.

It's been a tough few months.

Facing them—Doc, Happy, and Dumbass—was way more difficult than she thought it would be. Reliving all the lies. The setup. The assaults. All the things those teachers did. It was horrible.

Now it's over, the buzz has died down, but things are still hard. Getting on track again, and facing the reality of a blind and crippled future—it's hard. Having a mother who's a drunk is hard too. Thinking about college, where sleeping people are everywhere . . . and a boyfriend, whose doubts and fears only come out in his dreams. Life in general . . . yeah. All of it.

Really.

Fucking.

Hard.

Janie and Cabe do the dishes together. Cabel washes, Janie dries. It feels so homey. She grips a plate tightly, wiping it with the towel. Thinking.

Wants to know if he'll voice his dream fears.

And so she blurts it out. "Do you ever think about what it'll be like? You know, if we stick together, and me all blind and hobbling around, dropping and breaking dishes 'cause I can't hold on to them. . . ." She puts the plate in the cupboard.

Cabel flicks his fingers at her, spraying her with water. Grinning. "Sure. I think I'm pretty lucky. I bet blind people have great sex. I'll even wear a blindfold so it's fair." He bumps his hips lightly against hers. She doesn't laugh. She steadies herself and then grabs a stainless steel skillet by the handle and starts drying it. Stares at her contorted reflection in it.

"Hey," Cabe says. He dries his hand on his shorts and then strokes Janie's cheek. "I was just joking around."

"I know." She sighs and puts the pan away. Throws the towel on the counter. "Come on. Let's go do something fun."

1:12 p.m.

She focuses her mind.

It's cold in the water, but the afternoon sun is warm on her face, her hair.

Janie bobs in place, knees bent, arms straight but not locked, trying to balance. The life vest knocks about her ears. Her well-toned arms are like sticks shooting from the vest's enormous sockets. Janie's glasses are safely stowed inside the boat, so everything is blurry. It's like looking through a wall of rain.

She takes a deep breath. "Hit it!" she yells, and then she is yanked forward, knees knocking, arms shaking. She grips the rope handle, knuckles white, palms and muscles already sore from two previous days' efforts. *Lean back*, she remembers, and does it. *Let the boat pull you up.*

She straightens, sort of.

Wobbles and catches herself.

Her bum sticks out, she knows. But she can't help it. Doesn't care, anyway. All she can do is grin blindly as spray slaps and stings her face.

She's up. "Woo hoo!" she yells.

Megan is a gentle driver at the wheel of the little pea-green speedboat. She watches Janie in the rearview mirror like the good mothers watch their children, her brow furrowed in concern but nodding her head. Smiling.

Cabel faces Janie, in the spotter position at the back of the boat, grinning like he does. His teeth gleam white next to his tan skin, and his brown hair, streaked with gold from the sunshine, flips wildly in the wind. His nubbly burn scars on his belly and chest shine silvery brown.

But they are both just blobs to Janie from seventy-five feet away. Cabe yells something that sounds enthusiastic but it's lost in the noise of the motor and the splash.

Janie's legs and arms shiver as they air-dry and then get slapped with spray again. Her skin buzzes.

Megan keeps them close to the willow-treed shore. As they approach the town's beach and campground, Megan eases the boat into a wide semicircle, turning them around. Janie tenses into the turn, but it's only a mild bump over the wake. Once they straighten out again, Janie moistens her lips, and then, determined, she gives Megan the thumbs-up.

Faster.

Megan complies, and speeds toward the dock near the little red-brown shellacked cabin, one of six dotting the shore at the Rustic Logs Resort, and then she continues past it. Exploring new territory.

I am such a badass, Janie thinks. She squints and makes a daring and ultimately successful attempt to cross the wake again as the two in the boat cheer her on.

By the time Janie senses it, it's already too late.

A woman lies sunning herself on a water trampoline, skin gleaming from tanning oil and sweat. Janie can't make out the scene, but she's all too familiar with the warning signs. Her stomach twists.

Janie flies past the woman and becomes engulfed in darkness. There's a three-second-flash of a dream before it's all over and she's out of range again. But it's enough to throw Janie off-kilter. Her knees buckle, skis tangle underneath her, and she flips forward wildly, water forcing its way into her throat and nostrils. Into her brain, it seems, by the way it burns. A ski slams into her head and she's forced back under the water. She's not slowing down.

If you fall, let go of the rope.

Der.

Janie surfaces, coughing and sputtering, her head on fire. Amazed that the oversize life vest is still attached, though she's all twisted up in it. Feels queasy after swallowing half the lake. She wipes the water from her stinging eyes and peers through the blur, disoriented, wishing for her glasses. Ears plugged. When weeds suddenly tickle her dangling feet, she *eep*s and her body does a little freak-out spasm of oogy-ness, after which she tries not to think about being surrounded by big yellow-orange carp . . . and their excrement.

Blurg. Not fond of this, hello.

Boats whine in the distance.

None of them sounds like it is coming to rescue her.

Finally she hears a muffled chugging. When the motor cuts, Janie calls out. "Cabe?"

It's still the only name that feels safe on her tongue.

1:29 p.m.

In the boat, Cabel wraps a towel around her. Hands Janie her glasses. "You sure you're okay?" His eyes crinkle and he's trying not to grin.

"Fine," Janie growls, peeved, teeth chattering. Megan checks out the bump on Janie's head, and then hauls in the tow rope.

Cabel coughs lightly and then presses his lips together. "That was quite, uh, quite the display, Hannagan."

"Are you actually laughing at me? Seriously?" Janie rubs her hair with a towel. "I almost died out there. Plus my brain is now infested with plankton and carp shit. You'd better watch it, or I'll blow a snot rocket at you."

"I'm . . . eww. That's disgusting." Cabe laughs. "But seriously, you really should have seen yourself. Right, Megan? I wish we had a video camera."

"Dude, I am so Switzerland," Megan says. Rope stowed, she revs up the engine and swings the boat around, back to the dock.

For the second time today, Janie's not laughing.

Cabel continues over the noise. "I mean, the flip was one thing, but the drag, that was something entirely out of control. Your legs were flying. Remember rule number one of water skiing?"

"I know. Sheesh. When you fall, let go of the rope, I

know. There's just a lot of shit to remember when you're out there."

Cabel snorts. "A lot . . . yeah, a whole lot of shit to remember." He laughs long and hard, wipes his eyes and tries to get control of himself. "Shouldn't 'let go of the rope if it's drowning you' be sort of an automatic response, though? Basic survival technique?"

She glares at him.

He stops laughing and gives her a helpless, innocent look. "Okay, okay, I'm sorry," he says.

"Go suck a mean one," Janie says. She turns away and squints through her glasses, locating the sleeping woman on the trampoline, now a tiny island in the distance. *You still don't catch it all, do you, Cabe?*

He probably never will.

"Get over yourself, Hannagan," she mutters. "You're on vacation, damn it. You're relaxing and having fun." It sounds wooden.

"What's that, sweets?" He slides over to her on the bench seat.

"I said, it *was* kinda funny, wasn't it?" Janie looks into Cabel's eyes. Smiles sheepishly.

With his finger, he catches a drip of water from her chin. Smiles. He brings his finger to his lips and licks the water. "Mmm," he says, nuzzling her neck. "Carp shit."

1:53 p.m.

Cabel nods off on a blanket under a shady oak.

Janie sits, chin on her knees, staring at her toes. Listening to the rhythm of the soft waves washing up on shore. After a while, she gets up. "I'm going for a walk," she whispers. Cabel doesn't move.

She slips a long T-shirt over her swimsuit, shoves her toes in her flips, grabs her cell phone, and walks behind the cabin and through the little parking lot, up the steep driveway to the main road. Across the road there's a field and a railroad track. The rails glint in the late afternoon sunshine. Janie walks along the track and thinks, glad to have a quiet place where she can let her dream guard down.

After a while, she stops walking. Sits on the track, feeling the hot metal against the backs of her thighs through the thin cover-up. Opens her phone and dials memory #2.

"Janie—what's going on? Everything all right?"

Janie gently waves a bumblebee away. "Hi. Yeah. I'm just doing a lot of thinking. About what we talked about . . . you know? Lots of time to think on vacation," she says, and laughs nervously.

"And?"

"And . . . you're sure you are okay with whatever I decide?"

"Of course. You know that. Did you make up your mind, then?

"Not really. I'm—I'm still deciding."

"Have you talked to Cabel about it?"

Janie winces. "No. Not yet."

"Well, I don't blame you for wanting—and needing—to consider all of your options."

Janie's throat grows tight. "Thank you, sir."

"You know the drill. Call me anytime. Let me know what you choose."

"I will." Janie closes the phone and stares at it.

There's nothing more to say.

On the way back, she picks up a train-flattened penny from the track and wonders if one of the vacationers down the hill placed it there. Wonders if some excited little kid will come back for it. She sets it on the railroad tie so whoever it is will be sure to see it. Walks slowly back to the cabin to drop off her stuff. And then it's back outside, under the tree.

She watches Cabe sleep. Later, she dozes too, whenever she can get a chance while she wearily dodges Cabel's dreams, and the dreams of a sleeping child somewhere, probably in the cabin next door.

There is no getting away from it all here. Or anywhere.

No escape for her.

5:49 p.m.

A whistle blasts and the train rushes past up at the top of the hill. Everyone who was sleeping awakes.

"Another busy day at the lake," Cabel murmurs. "My stomach's growling." He rolls over on the blanket. Janie can't resist. She snuggles up to his warm body.

"I can hear it," she says. "And I smell the charcoal grill."

"We should really get up now."

"I know."

They remain still, Janie's head on Cabel's chest, a nice breeze coming off the lake. She squinches her eyes shut and holds him, takes in the scent of him, feels the warmth of his chest on her cheek. Loves him.

Breaks a little more inside.

6:25 p.m.

Janie hears the click of the cabin's screen door and sits up guiltily as Megan walks over to them. "I'm sorry, Megan—we should be helping you get dinner."

"Nah," Megan grins. "You needed a nap after all that skiing and drowning. But your cell phone is beeping inside the cabin. I don't know what to do with it."

"Thanks. I'll check it."

Cabel sits up too. "Everything okay? Where's Charlie, anyway?"

"In town picking up some groceries. It's all good.

Relax," Megan says. "Seriously. It's been a tough time for you guys—you need the rest."

Obediently, Cabel sinks back down on the blanket as Janie gets to her feet. "Be right back," she says. "It better not be Captain with an assignment or I'm quitting."

Cabel laughs. "You wouldn't."

6:29 p.m.

Voicemails.

From Carrie. Five of them.

And they're bad.

Janie listens, incredulous. Listens again, stunned.

"Hey, Janers, dammit, where are you? Call me." *Click.*

"Janie, seriously. There's something wrong with your mom. Call me." *Click.*

"Janie, seriously! Your mom is stumbling around your front yard yelling for you. Didn't you tell her you were going to Fremont? She's totally drunk, Janie—she's wailing and—oh, shit. She's in the road." *Click.*

"Hey. I'm taking your mom to County Hospital. If she blows in Ethel, you are so dead. Call me. Jesus. Also? Shit. My phone battery is dying, so maybe try the hospital or something . . . don't know what to tell you. I'll try you *again* when I have a chance." *Click.*

"Oh, my God." Janie stares at her phone, not really seeing it. Then she calls Carrie.

Gets Carrie's voice mail. "Carrie! What happened? Call me. I've got my phone now. I'm so sorry. I was— taking a nap." It sounds hollow. Careless. Frivolous, even, when Janie says it aloud. *What was I thinking, leaving my mother alone for a week?* "God. Just call me."

Janie stands there, all the breath being sucked out of her, replaced by fear. *What if something's really wrong?*

And then anger.

I will never have a life as long as that woman is alive, she thinks.

Squeezes her eyes shut and takes it back, immediately.

Can't believe she would be such a horrible person, think such a horrible thing.

Charlie walks into the tiny cabin kitchen with a brown bag of groceries and stops short when he sees the look on Janie's face. "Are you okay?" he asks.

Janie blinks, unsure. "No, I don't think so," she says quietly. "I think . . . I think I have to go."

Charlie sets the groceries down hard on the counter. "Cabe!" he shouts through the screen door. "Come 'ere."

Janie sets her phone down and pulls her suitcase from the wardrobe. Starts throwing her clothes in her suitcase. She looks at her disheveled self in the mirror and rakes her fingers through her dark blond tangles. "Oh, my God," she says to herself. "What the hell is wrong with my mother?"

And then it hits.

What if her mother really is dying? Or dead?

It's both fascinating and horrifying. Janie imagines the scene.

"What is it?" Cabel says, coming into the cabin. "What's going on?"

"Here," she says. She dials voice mail and hands the phone to Cabel. "Listen to all the messages."

As Cabel listens, Janie, in a daze, continues to pack.

After all her things are crammed inside, she realizes that she needs something to change into—she can't drive all the way to Fieldridge in her swimsuit.

She can't drive at all.

Cue major detail.

"Fuck," Janie mutters. She watches as Cabel listens to the messages. Watches his expression intensify.

"Holy shit," he says. He looks at Janie. Takes her hand. "Holy shit, Janie. What can I do?"

Janie just buries her face in his neck. Trying not to think.

Endless.

7:03 p.m.

It's a three-hour drive home. Cabel's at the wheel of the Beemer that Captain Komisky lets him drive. A Grand Rapids radio station deejay cracks a lame joke and then plays Danny Reyes's "Bleecker Street" in his all-request hour, and Janie stares at her phone, willing Carrie to call. But it's silent.

Janie calls the hospital. They have no record of a Dorothea Hannagan being admitted.

"Maybe she's fine and they didn't have to admit her," Cabel says.

"Or maybe she's in the morgue."

"They'd have called you by now."

Janie's silent, trying to think of reasons why the hospital hasn't called, much less Carrie with an update.

"We can call Captain," Cabel says.

"What good will that do?"

"The police chief? She can get info from anybody she wants."

"True. But . . ." Janie sighs. "I don't . . . my mother . . . never mind. No. I don't want to call Captain."

"Why? It would put your mind at ease."

"Cabe . . ."

"Janie, seriously. You should call her—get the scoop. She'd totally do it for you if you're worried about imposing."

"No thanks."

"You want me to call her?"

"No. Okay? I don't want her to know."

Cabel sighs, exasperated. "I don't get it."

Janie clenches her jaw. Looks out the window. Feels the heat in her cheeks, the tears stinging. The shame. Says softly, "It's embarrassing, all right? My mom's a freaking drunk. Stumbling around in the front yard, yelling? My God. I just don't need Captain seeing that. Or knowing about that—that part of my life. It's personal. There are things I talk about with Captain, and things that are private. Just drop it."

Cabel is silent. After a few minutes of radio dee-jay babble, he plugs his iPod into the car stereo. Josh Schicker's "Feels Like Rain" washes through the car. When the song ends and the first notes of the next song begin, he stiffens and then hastily flips it off. Knows what's next. Knows it's "Good Mothers, Don't Leave!"

An hour passes as they travel eastward across Michigan, leaving the sun setting orange and bright in their wake. Traffic is light. Janie leans her head against the window, watching the blur of deep green trees and yellow fields pass by. There's a deer in a grassy area as darkness approaches—or maybe it's just that burned-out tree stump that fools her every time.

She wonders how many more times she'll witness

scenes like this. Trying to remember everything she sees now, for later. When all she has is darkness and dreams.

She tries the hospital again. Still no record of Dorothea Hannagan. It's a good sign, Janie thinks . . . except that Carrie still isn't calling. "Where is she?" Janie bounces her head against the headrest.

Cabel glances sidelong at Janie. "Carrie? Didn't she say her phone's dead?"

"She said her battery was low. But there are other phones. . . ."

Cabel taps his chin thoughtfully. "Does she actually know your cell number or are you on her speed dial?"

"Ahh. Good point. Speed dial."

"So that's why she hasn't called. She doesn't know your number, it's in her dead phone and she can't get to it."

Janie smiles. Lets go of a worried breath. "Yeah . . . you're probably right."

"Did you try calling your house to see if your mom is there?"

"Yeah, I did that, too. No answer."

"Do you have Stu's number? Or Carrie's home phone?"

"I tried her home. No answer. And I don't have Stu's. I should. I've always meant to. . . ."

"What about Melinda?"

"Yeah, right." Janie snorts. "Just what I need—the knobs from the Hill spreading this story around." She turns back to the window. "I'm sorry I was snippy. You know—earlier."

Cabel smiles in the darkness. "S'okay." He reaches for Janie's hand. Snakes his fingers between hers. "I wasn't thinking. My bad." He pauses. "You know nobody thinks badly of you for things you can't control, like what your mother does."

"Nobody?" Janie scowls. "Right. They all have their opinion on the Durbin mess."

"Nobody who matters."

Janie tilts her head. "Yanno, Cabe, maybe neighbors, the entire town of Fieldridge . . . maybe what they think actually does matter to me. I mean, God. Forget it. I'm just so tired of all of this. Sheesh, what next?"

After a pause, Cabel says, "Straight to the hospital, then, right?"

"Yeah, I figure that's the best thing we can do. She could just be sitting, waiting in the ER. We'll try that first . . . you think?"

"Yeah."

9:57 p.m.

Janie and Cabel stand in the ER, unsure of what to do. No sign of Carrie or Janie's mother anywhere among the assortment of ill and injured. No one at the desk has any record of her either.

Cabel taps his fingers against his lips, thinking. "Is Hannagan your mom's married name?"

Janie squinches her eyes shut and sighs. "No." She's never told Cabel much about her mother, and he's never asked. Which was just the way Janie liked it. Until now.

"Um . . . ?" Cabel prompts. "How do I put this PC. Let's see. Okay, has your mom ever gone by any other name besides Hannagan?"

"No. Her name's Dorothea Hannagan, and that's the only name she's ever had. I'm a bastard. Okay?"

"Janie, seriously. Nobody cares about that."

"Yeah, well, I care. At least you know who both your parents are."

Cabel stares at Janie. "Fat lot of good that did me."

"Oh, jeez, Cabe." Janie grimaces. "I'm sorry. Major verbal typo. I'm stressed—I don't know what I'm saying."

Cabel looks like he's about to say something, but he holds back. Looks around again, futilely. "Come on," he says, grabbing Janie's hand. "Elevator. We'll walk around, check waiting rooms. Ten minutes, tops, and if we don't find Carrie, we head back to your house and wait. I don't know what else to do."

A shiver crawls over Janie's skin. Her mother, the drunk, is missing.

10:02 p.m.

There, in the third-floor waiting room.

ICU.

Elbows on her knees and face in her hands, fingers threaded through her long dark curls. Leaning forward. Like she's ready to jump to her feet at any second and run like hell.

"Carrie!" Janie says.

Carrie pops up. "Oh, good, you got my note."

"Where's . . . Is my mother . . . ?"

"She's in the room with him."

"What? Who?"

"Didn't you get my note?"

"What note? All I know is what you left on my voice mail."

"I left a note on Ethel—in the parking lot. Figured you're a detective now, or whatever. You oughta think to look for my car. Anyways, how the hell did you find me, then? Never mind. Your mom—she's fine. I mean, she's still drunk but I think she's coming down now . . . like way down. She's all weepy and shaky. But—"

"Carrie," Janie says firmly. "Focus. Tell me what's wrong with my mother and where I can find her."

Carrie sighs. She looks tired. "Your mom is fine. Just drunk."

Janie glances nervously through the open door to the

hallway as a nurse walks by. Her voice is low and urgent. "Okay, okay, I get that she's drunk. She's always drunk. Can we stop shouting that please? And if she's fine, why the fuck are we all in Intensive Care?"

"Oh, man," Carrie says. She shakes her head. "Where to start?"

Cabel nudges Janie and Carrie toward the chairs and sits down with them. "Who's 'him', Carrie? Who is she with?" he says gently.

Janie nods, echoing the question.

But she already knows.

There's only one "him" it could possibly be. There is no one else in the world. No one else that would make Janie's mother react this way. No one else Janie's mother dreams about.

Carrie, whose normally dancing eyes are dulled from the weariness of the unusual day, looks at Janie. "Apparently, it's your father, Janers. He's, like, really sick."

Janie just looks at Carrie. "My father?"

"They don't think he's going to make it."

10:06 p.m.

Janie falls back into the chair. Numb. No idea how she's supposed to feel about this news. No. Freaking. Clue.

Cabel lifts his hand to pause the conversation. The three sit in the waiting room in silence for a moment, Janie looking blank, Carrie working a piece of gum, Cabel closing his eyes and shaking his head ever so slightly. "Start from the beginning," he says.

Carrie nods. Thinks. "Yeah, so, this afternoon, probably around three o'clock, I heard somebody hollering outside. I ignored it 'cause there's always somebody yelling around our neighborhood, right? And I'm folding laundry on the bed and then through my window I see Janie's mom, which is so weird, because she, like, never goes outside unless she's walking to the gas station or the bus stop to get booze, right? But today she's in her nightgown wandering around the yard—"

Janie flushes and puts her hands to her face. "Oh, God," she says.

"—and, uh, she's calling 'Janie! Janie!' and then she sort of stumbles and I go running outside to see what's wrong with her. And Dorothea, she's crying and says, 'The phone! I gotta go to the hospital,' over and over about twenty times, and I'm calling you and leaving you messages and finally I just drive her here 'cause I don't know what else to do. And it takes us like an hour of sitting in the ER and talking to the receptionist before she's . . . um . . . calmed down and able to explain that she's not sick—that she got a phone call and she needs to see Henry."

Janie looks up. "Henry?"

"Yeah, Henry Feingold. That's the guy's name."

"Henry Feingold," Janie says. The name sounds empty. It has no meaning to her. It doesn't sound like what she imagined her father's name would be. "How would I even know if that's him? Dorothea," she says, emphasizing each syllable, "never bothered to share any information with me about him."

Carrie nods solemnly. She knows.

And then.

Janie blinks back the tears as she realizes the truth. "He must live nearby if they brought him here. Guess he didn't ever bother to know me, either."

"I'm sorry, hon." Carrie looks at the floor.

Janie stands abruptly and turns to Cabel and Carrie. "I can't believe she ruined our vacation. And I'm so sorry, Carrie, that you wasted your whole day and evening here. You are such a good friend—please, go on home or to Stu's or whatever."

She turns to Cabel. "Cabe, I'll handle this from here. I'll take the bus home once I collect my mother. Please, guys. Go get some rest." She walks toward the door, hoping Carrie and Cabe will follow so she can usher them out and suffer the embarrassment of all of this in private. Her bottom lip quivers. *God, this is so fucked up.*

Cabel stands up, and then Carrie stands too. "So," Cabel says to Carrie as they follow Janie to the door. "What's wrong with him? Do you know?"

"Some brain injury or something. I don't know much—I heard the doc tell Dorothea that he called 911 and was still conscious until after he got here, but now he won't wake up. They finally let Dorothea in to see him about thirty minutes ago. And Janers," Carrie says, "it was no problem, okay? You'd do the same if my mom needed help. Right?"

Janie's throat tightens and she blinks back the tears. All she can do is nod. When Carrie hugs her, Janie chokes back a sob. "Thanks," Janie whispers in Carrie's hair.

Carrie turns to go. "Call me."

Janie nods again, watching Carrie walk to the elevators. And then she looks at Cabel. "Go," she says.

"No."

He's not going anywhere.

Janie sighs uneasily. Because it's great he's so supportive, but this situation is totally weird. And Janie's not quite sure what to expect.

Some things are really just easier done alone.

It's quiet and the lights are low as Janie and Cabel push through the double doors into the ICU patients' hallway. Janie feels the faint pull of a dream from a distance and she combats it immediately, impatiently. Spies the culprit's room whose door stands ajar and silently curses him. Frustrated she can't ever get away from people's dreams, even when her mind is extremely busy doing other things.

They check in at the nurses' station. Janie clears her throat. "Henry, uh, Fein . . . stei—"

"Feingold," Cabel says smoothly.

"Are you family?" the nurse asks. She looks at them suspiciously.

"I, uh," Janie says. "Yeah. He's my . . . father . . . I guess."

The nurse cocks her head to the side. "The trick to getting into someone's room is to lie *convincingly*," she says. "Nice try."

"I—I don't want to go into his room. Just tell my mother I'm here, will you? She's in there with him. I'll be in the waiting room." Janie turns around abruptly and Cabel shrugs at the nurse and follows. They march back through the double doors to the waiting room, leaving a puzzled nurse watching them go.

Janie mutters under her breath as she flings herself in a chair. "Feingold. Harvey Feingold."

Cabe glances at her. "Henry."

"Right. Jeez. You'd never guess I work for the cops."

"Which is probably why you're so convincing under-cover," Cabel says, grinning.

Janie elbows him automatically. "Well, not anymore. Don't forget you're talking to narc girl." She turns to him.

Grabs his hand. Implores. "Cabe, really, you should go. Get some sleep. Go back to Fremont and enjoy the rest of the week. I'm fine here. I can handle this."

Cabel regards Janie and sighs. "I know you can handle it, Janie. You're such a damn martyr. It's tiring, really, having this same argument with you every time you've got shit happening. Just let it go. I'm not leaving." He smiles faux-diplomatically.

Janie's jaw drops. "A martyr!"

"Ahh, yeah. Slightly."

"Please. You can't be *slightly* a martyr. You either are, or you aren't. It's like *unique*."

Cabel laughs softly, the corners of his eyes crinkling. And then he just gazes at her, smiling the crooked smile that Janie remembers from the awkward skateboard days.

But right now, Janie can't seem to smile back.

"Um, about this little adventure," she begins. "This is really mortifying, Cabe. I'm . . . I'm so embarrassed about it, and I have a lot on my mind, and I can hardly stand how nice you are being. I hate that I'm ruining your time too, instead of just my own. So, really, please. It would make me feel better if you'd just, you know . . ." Janie gives him a helpless look.

Cabel blinks.

His forehead crinkles and he looks earnestly at her.

"Ahh," he says. "You really do want me to go home.

When you say this is embarrassing, you mean it's embarrassing to you for *me* to know this stuff too?"

Janie looks at the floor, giving him the answer.

"Oh." Cabel measures his words, stung. "I'm sorry, Janers. I didn't pick up on that." He gets up quickly. Walks to the door. Janie follows him to the hallway by the elevators. "I'll . . . I'll see you around, I guess," he says. "Call me when—whenever."

"I will," Janie says, staring at the big CELL PHONES MUST BE TURNED OFF sign on the wall. "I'll text you later. This is just really something I'd rather handle alone at the moment, okay? I love you."

"Yeah. Okay. Love you, too." Cabel swivels on his flips and waves an uncertain hand at her. He looks over his shoulder. "Hey? Bus doesn't run between two and five a.m., you know that, right?"

Janie smiles. "I know."

"Don't get sucked into any dreams, okay?"

"Okay. Shh." Janie says, hoping no one else heard that.

Before he can think of anything else, Janie slips back inside the waiting room to sit and think.

Alone.

1:12 a.m.

She dozes in the waiting room chair.

Suddenly feels someone watching her. Startles and sits up, awake.

At least her mother is wearing clothes and not the nightgown Carrie mentioned.

"Hey," Janie says. She stands. Walks over to her mother and stops, feeling awkward. Not sure what to do. Hug? That's what they do on TV. Weirdness.

Dorothea Hannagan is sweating profusely. Shaking. Janie doesn't want to touch her. This whole scene is so foreign it's almost otherworldly.

And then.

Madness.

"Where were you?" Janie's mother crumples and she starts crying. Yelling too loud. "You don't tell me nothing about where you are, you just disappear. That strange girl from next door has to drive me here—" Her hands are shaking and her shifty eyes dart from the floor back up to Janie's, accusing, angry. "You don't care about your mother now, is that it? You just running around wild with that boy?"

Janie steps back, stunned, not just at the sheer record number of words uttered by her mother in one day, but even more by the tone. "Oh, my God."

"Don't you talk back to me." Dorothea's shaking hands rip open her ragged vinyl purse and she rifles through it, dumping wrappers and papers onto the waiting room chairs. It becomes painfully obvious that what she's looking for is not there. Dorothea gives up and slumps in a chair.

Janie, standing, watches.

She's shaking a little bit too.

Wondering how to handle this. And why she has to. *Haven't you given me enough shit to deal with already?* she says to no one. Or maybe to God. She doesn't know. But she does know one thing. She'll be glad to be away from this mess.

Janie picks up the scattered objects from the waiting room, shoves them into the purse, and takes her mother by the arm. "Come on. You've got some at the house, right?"

Janie tugs Dorothea to her feet. "I said, come on. We have to catch the bus."

"What about your car?" Dorothea asks. "That girl was driving it."

Janie blinks and looks at her mother, dragging her along to the elevator. "Yeah, Ma. I sold it to her months ago, remember?"

"You never tell me—"

"Just . . ." Janie burns. *I don't tell you anything? Or you're too drunk to remember?* She takes a breath, lets it out slowly. "Just come on. And don't embarrass me."

"Yeah, well don't you embarrass me, either."

"Whatever."

Janie gives a fleeting glance over her shoulder down the hallway where presumably her father lies, dead or alive, Janie doesn't know.

Doesn't really care.

Hopes he hurries up and dies so she doesn't ever have to deal with him. Because from all Janie knows, parents are nothing but trouble.

2:10 a.m.

Dorothea fidgets like a junkie the entire way home on the bus. Janie, frustrated, wards off the dream of a homeless passenger and is just glad it's a short ride.

When they get home, there on the front step is Janie's suitcase. "Damn, Cabe," she mutters. "Why do you always have to be so fucking thoughtful?"

Janie's mother makes a beeline to the kitchen, grabs a bottle of vodka from under the sink, and retreats to her bedroom without a word. Janie lets her go. There will be time tomorrow to figure out what's going on with this Henry person once Dorothea is good and sloshed and halfway reasonable again.

Janie texts Cabel.

Home.

Cabe responds without delay, despite the hour.

Thx baby. Love. See you tomorrow?

Turns off her phone. "Yeah, about that," Janie whispers. She sighs and sets the phone on her bedside table and her suitcase next to it, and falls into bed.

4:24 a.m.

Janie dreams.

There are rocks covering her bedroom floor and a suitcase on her bed. Each rock has something scribbled on it, but Janie can only read the rocks when she picks them up.

She picks one. "HELP ME," it reads. "CABE," reads another.

"DOROTHEA. CRIPPLED. SECRET. BLIND."

When she puts them back on the floor, they grow bigger, heavier. Soon, she knows, she will run out of room on the floor to put the rocks, but she can't stop picking them up, reading them. The floor is crowded, and Janie's having trouble breathing. The rocks are sucking the air from the room.

Finally, Janie sets a rock in the suitcase. It shrinks to the size of a pebble.

Janie slowly, methodically, picks up all the rocks and puts them in the suitcase. The task seems endless. Finally, she picks up the last one, "ISOLATE." Sets it down with the others. It becomes a pebble, and all the other pebbles disappear.

Janie stares at the suitcase. Knows what she has to do.

She closes it.
Picks it up.
And walks out.

FRIDAY

August 4, 2006, 9:15 a.m.

Janie lies awake, staring at the ceiling. Thinking about everything. About this one more thing. The green notebook, the hearing, the gossip, college, her mother, and now this guy Henry. What's next? It's too much already. A familiar wave of panic washes over her, captures her chest and squeezes it. Hard. Harder. Janie gulps for air and she can't get enough. She rolls to her side in a ball.

"Chill," she says, gasping. "Just chill the fuck out."

It's all too much.

She covers her mouth and nose with her hands, breathes into them, in and out, until she can get a good breath. She makes her mind go blank.

Focuses.

Breathes.

Just breathes.

9:29 a.m.

The door to Janie's mother's room remains closed.

Janie wanders aimlessly around the little house, wondering what the hell she's supposed to do about Henry. She nibbles on a granola bar, sweating. It's a scorcher already. She flips on the oscillating fan in the living room and props open the front door, begging for a breeze, and then she plops down on the couch.

Through the ripped screen door Janie sees Cabel pulling into the driveway, and her heart sinks. He hops out of the car and takes long, smooth strides to the front door. Lets himself in, as usual. He stops and lets his eyes adjust.

Smiles a crooked smile. "Hey," he says.

She pats the worn couch cushion next to her. "I haven't brushed my teeth yet," she says as Cabel leans in. "Your nose is peeling."

"Don't care, and don't care." Cabel leans in and kisses her. Then he plops down on the couch. "You okay that I'm here . . . and stuff?" he asks.

"Yeah." Janie slides her hand on his thigh and squeezes.

"Last night . . . I just didn't know what to expect. I wasn't sure about my mom, you know? Wasn't sure what she'd do."

"What *did* she do?" He looks around nervously.

"Not much. She was a little obnoxious. Not impossible. But she didn't say a word about Henry and I didn't dare ask. God, she can't even go twelve hours without a drink. And if she doesn't have one, she gets mean." Janie drops her chin. "It's embarrassing, you know?"

"My dad was like that too. Only he was mean with or without. At least he was consistent." Cabel grins wryly.

Janie snorts. "I guess I'm lucky." She glances sidelong at Cabel.

Considers.

Finally says, "Did you ever wish your dad was dead? I mean, before he hurt you? Just so you could, like, not have to deal with him anymore?"

Cabel narrows his eyes. "Every. Damn. Day."

Janie bites her lip. "So, are you glad he died in jail?"

Cabel is quiet for a long time. Then he shrugs. When he speaks, his voice is measured, almost clinical, as if he is talking to a shrink. "It was the best possible outcome, under the circumstances."

The fan blows a knee-level path from the TV to the coffee table, catching the two pairs of bare legs on the couch in the middle of its run. Janie shivers slightly when the air hits her sweat-dampened skin. She thinks of Henry

Feingold, the stranger, presumably her father. Dying. And for the third time in twenty-four hours, Janie wishes it were someone else.

She leans her head against Cabel's shoulder and slips her arm behind his. He turns, slides her onto his lap, and they hold on tightly to each other.

Because there's no one else.

She's so conflicted.

Janie imagines life without people. Without him. Broken heart, loneliness, but able to see, to feel. To live. To be, in peace. Not always looking over her shoulder for the next dream attack.

And she imagines life with him. Blind, gnarled, but loved . . . at least while things are still good. And always knowing what struggles he's dealing with through his dreams. Does she really want to see that, as years go by? Does she really want to be this incredible burden to such an awesome guy?

She still doesn't know which scenario wins.

But she's thinking.

Maybe broken hearts can mend more easily than broken hands and eyes.

9:41 a.m.

It's too hot to sit like that for long.

Cabe stretches. "You going to wake her up? Head down to the hospital again?"

"God, I hope not."

"Janie."

"Yeah, I know."

"At least it's air-conditioned there."

"So's your car. Wanna go make out in the driveway instead?"

Cabel laughs. "Maybe after dark. In fact, hell yes, after dark. But seriously, Janie. I think you need to talk to your mom."

Janie sighs and rolls her eyes. "I suppose."

9:49 a.m.

She taps softly on her mother's bedroom door.

Glances at Cabel.

To Janie, this room doesn't feel like a part of the house. It's more just a door to another world, a portal to sorrow, from which Dorothea appears and disappears at random. Rarely does she even catch a glimpse inside unless her mother is coming or going.

She waits. Enters, bracing herself against a possible dream. But Janie's mother isn't dreaming at the moment. Janie lets out a breath and looks around.

Filtered sunlight squeezes into the room through the worn patches of the window drape. The furnishings are spare but what's there is messy. Paper plates, bottles, and glasses are on the floor next to the bed. It's hot and stuffy. Stale.

In the bed, Janie's mother sleeps on her back, the thin nightgown gripping her bony figure.

"Mom," Janie whispers.

There's no response.

Janie feels self-conscious. She shifts on the balls of her feet. The floor creaks. "Mother," she says, louder this time.

Janie's mother grunts and looks up, squinting. Hoists herself with effort on her elbow. "Issit the phone?" she mumbles.

"No, I . . . it's almost ten o'clock and I was just wondering—"

"Don't you got school?"

Janie's jaw drops. *You've got to be kidding me.* She takes a deep breath, considers blowing up at her mother, reminding her of the graduation she didn't attend, and the fact that it's summer, but decides now is not the time. The words rush out before Dorothea can interrupt again. "No, ah, no school today. I'm wondering what the deal is with Henry and if you have to go to the hospital again or what. I don't want to—"

At the mention of Henry, Janie's mother sucks in a loud breath. "Oh, my God," she says, moaning, as if she just remembered what happened. She rolls over and shakily gets to her feet. Shuffles past Janie, out of the bedroom. Janie follows.

"Mom?" Janie doesn't know what to do. As they turn toward the kitchen, Janie gives Cabel a helpless look and he shrugs. "Mother."

Dorothea pulls orange juice from the fridge, ice and vodka from the freezer, and pours herself some breakfast. "What?" she asks, sniffling.

"Is this Henry guy my father?"

"Of course he's your father. I'm no whore."

Cabel makes a muffled noise from the other room.

"Okay, so he's dying?"

Janie's mother takes a long drink from the glass. "That's what they say."

"Well, was he in an accident or is it a disease or what?"

Dorothea shrugs and waves her hand loosely. "His brain exploded. Or a tumor. Something."

Janie sighs. "Do you need me to go with you to the hospital again today?"

For the first time in the conversation, Janie's mother looks Janie in the eye. "Again? You didn't go with me yesterday."

"I got there as soon as I could, Ma."

Janie's mother drains the glass and shudders. She

stands at the counter, one hand holding the empty glass, the other holding the bottle of cheap vodka, and she stares at it. She sets both glass and bottle down hard and closes her eyes. A tear escapes and runs down her cheek.

Janie rolls her eyes. "You going to the hospital or not? I'm"—she grows bold—"I'm not sitting around all day waiting."

"Go do whatever you want, like you always do, you little tramp," Dorothea says. "I'm not going back there anyways." She shuffles unsteadily past Janie, down the hall and into her room, closing the door once more behind her.

Janie lets out a breath and moves back into the living room where Cabel sits, a witness to it all. "Okay," she says. "Now what?"

Cabel looks peeved. He shakes his head. "Well, what do you think you should do?"

"I'm not going back to see him, if that's what you're asking."

"Me? Of course not. It's totally up to you if you want to see the guy."

"Right. Good."

"I mean, he's a deadbeat dad. Never done a thing for you. Who knows, maybe he has another family. Think of how awkward that would be if you just showed up and they were all there. . . ." Cabel trails off.

"Yeah, God, I never thought of that."

"I'm trying to think if there were any Feingolds at Fieldridge High. Maybe you have half-siblings, you know?"

"There's that one guy, Josh, that freshman who played varsity basketball," Janie says.

"That's Feinstein."

"Oh."

And then there is a moment, a pause, as Cabel waits for Janie.

"So, Feingold, that's Jewish, right?" she asks.

"Does that change anything if it is?"

"No. I mean, wow. It's interesting, anyway. I never really thought about my roots, you know? History. Ancestors. Wow." Janie's lost in thought.

Cabel nods. "Ah, well. You'll never know, I guess."

Janie freezes and then looks at Cabel.

Winds up and slugs him in the arm.

Hard.

"Ugh!" she says. "You loser."

Cabel laughs, rubbing his arm. "Dang! What'd I do this time?"

Janie seethes, half-jokingly. She shakes her head. "You made me give a shit."

"Come on," he says. "You cared before. Didn't you ever wonder who your father was?"

Janie thinks about the recurring dream her mother has—the kaleidoscope one where Dorothea and the hippie guy hold hands, floating. She'd wondered more than once who her father was. Wonders now if that was Henry in the dream.

"He's probably some suit with two-point-two kids and a dog and a house by U of M." Janie looks around her crap-hole of a house. Her crap-hole life, playing mom to an alcoholic twice her age. Knowing that without Dorothea's welfare check and Janie's income to supplement it, they are just one step away from being homeless. But Janie doesn't want to think about that.

Janie takes a deep breath and lets it out slowly. "All right. I'm grabbing a shower now, and later I'll head over to the hospital. I suppose you're coming with me then?"

Cabel smiles. "'Course. I'm your driver, remember?"

11:29 a.m.

Cabel and Janie take the stairs up to the third floor. By the time they reach the double doors that lead to the ward, Janie's moving more and more slowly until she stops. She turns abruptly and goes into the waiting room instead.

"I can't do this," she says.

"You don't have to. But if you don't, I think you'll be pissed at yourself later."

"If he has any other visitors, I'm leaving."

"That's fair."

"What if . . . what if he's awake? What if he sees me?"

Cabel presses his lips together. "Well, after what your mother said about his brain exploding, I highly doubt that will happen."

Janie sighs deeply and again walks toward the double doors with Cabel following. "Okay." She pushes through and does an automatic cursory glance, like she used to do at Heather Home, to see if any of the patients' doors are open. Luckily, most are closed, and Janie's not picking up any dreams today.

Janie approaches the desk, this time with confidence. "Henry Feingold, please."

"Family only," the nurse says automatically. His name tag says "Miguel."

"I'm his daughter."

"Hey," he says, looking at her more carefully. "Aren't you that narc girl?"

"Yeah." Janie tries not to fidget visibly.

"I saw you on the news. You did a good job."

Janie smiles. "Thank you. So . . . what room?"

"Room three-twelve. End of the hall on the right." Miguel points at Cabel. "You?"

"He's—" Janie says. "He and I. We're together."

The nurse eyes Janie. "I see. So. He's your . . . brother?"

Janie lets out a small breath and smiles gratefully. "Yes."

Cabel nods and remains quiet, almost as if to prove to Miguel that he will behave despite being completely unrelated to anyone in the vicinity.

"Can you tell me what his condition is?"

"He's not conscious, hon. Doctor Ming will have to give you an update." Miguel gives Janie a look of sympathy. A look that says, "Things are not good."

"Thank you," Janie murmurs. She sets off down the hallway with Cabel close behind. And when she opens the door . . .

Static. The noise is like top-volume radio static. Janie drops to her knees and holds her ears, even though she knows that won't help. Bright colors fly around her, giant slabs of red and purple; a wave of yellow so shocking it feels like it burns her eyeballs. She tries to speak but she can't.

There's no one there. Just wretched static and blinding lights. It's so painful, so void of feeling or emotion, it's like nothing Janie's ever witnessed before.

With a huge effort, Janie concentrates and pulls hard. Just as she feels herself pulling away, the scene blinks and clears. For a split second, there's a woman standing in a huge, dark room, and a man sitting in a chair in the corner, fading as Janie closes the door on that nightmare.

Janie catches her breath and when she can see again and feel her extremities, finds herself on her hands and knees just inside the doorway of the room. Cabel's right there beside her, muttering something, but she's not paying attention. She stares at the tiles on the floor and wonders briefly if that dream, that chaos, is what hell might be like.

"I'm okay," she says to Cabel, slowly getting to her feet, dusting invisible floor-dirt particles from her bare knees.

And then she straightens. Turns.

Looks at the source of the nightmare, and sees him for the first time.

The man who is her father. Whose DNA she carries.

Janie sucks in a breath. Slowly, her hand goes to her mouth and she takes a step backward. Her eyes grow wide in horror.

"Oh, my God," she whispers. "What the hell is that?"

WHAT THE HELL IT IS

Still Friday, August 4, 2006, 11:40 a.m.

Cabel puts his arm around Janie's shoulders, whether to show support or to keep her from bolting from the room, Janie doesn't know. Doesn't care. She's too horrified to move.

"He looks like a cross between Captain Caveman and the Unabomber," she whispers.

Cabel nods slowly. "Whoa. That's some funky Alice Cooper frizz." He turns to look at Janie. Says, in a soft voice, "What was the dream like?"

Janie can't take her eyes off the thin, very hairy man in the bed. He's surrounded by machines, but none of them are attached, none turned on. He wears no casts, no bandages. No gauze or white tape.

Just a look of incredible agony on his face.

She glances at Cabel, answers his question. "It was a strange dream," Janie says. "I'm not even sure it was a dream. It was more like a nondream. Like . . . when you're watching TV and the cable goes out. You get that loud, static, fuzzy noise at full blast."

"Weird. Was it black-and-white dots, too?"

"No—colors. Like giant beams of incredibly bright colors—purple, red, yellow. Three-dimensional colored walls turning and coming at me, coming together to make a box and closing in on me, so bright I could hardly stand it. It was awful."

"I'm glad you got out of it."

Janie nods. "Then for a split second, the walls disappeared and there was a woman there, way at the end, but it was too late for me to see. I was already pulling out of it. It felt like I was about to glimpse a piece of a real dream, maybe."

"Can you go back in?"

"I don't know. I've never tried that," she says. "Maybe if I go out of the room, shut the door, and come back in. But I don't really think I want to, you know?"

Cabel nods. He takes a step closer to the man. Picks up the chart that dangles from the foot of the bed. Stares at it intently for a moment and flips the top page over to look at the next page. Hands it to Janie. "I don't really understand this stuff. You want to know what's going on?"

Janie takes the clipboard uncertainly, feeling like she's intruding on a stranger. Still, she looks at it. Tries to decipher the terminology. But even with her experience working at Heather Home, there's not much Janie can understand.

"Huh. Looks like they detected sporadic, mild brain activity."

"Mild? Is that good?" Cabel sounds worried.

"I don't think so," Janie says. She puts the chart back.

"Can he hear us?" Cabel whispers.

Janie's quiet for a moment. Then she whispers too. "It's possible. At Heather Home, we always talked to the Hospice coma patients as if they could hear us, and told the families to do it too. Just in case."

Cabel swallows hard and looks at Janie, suddenly tongue-tied. He nudges her and nods toward the bed.

Janie frowns. "Don't rush me," she whispers.

She peers at the man. Steps closer. A shiver overtakes her and she stops when she's just a step away from her grizzly father. *What if he's faking and he jumps up at me?* Janie shivers again.

She takes a deep breath, and for a moment, she's Janie Hannagan, undercover. Looks more closely at Henry's distressed expression. Under all the long, black facial hair his skin is rough. Pockmarked. Janie wonders if he's the one she has to thank for her occasional zitbreaks. The hair on his head is patchy and thin in spots—as if great bunches of it had been pulled out. In places, she can see Henry's scalp. It's covered in red scratches.

She looks at his hands. His fingernails are clean but chewed down to the quick. Little scabs dot his cuticles. The hair on his chest that protrudes from his hospital gown is also patchy and decidedly grayer than the hair on his head. His complexion is grayish-white, as if he hadn't seen much sun all summer, but his arms have a light farmer's tan line.

"What happened to you?" She whispers it, more to herself than to him.

He doesn't stir. Still, the look of agony on his face is more than a bit unsettling. She wonders if the static is still going on in his mind. "That must be very painful," she murmurs.

Abruptly she looks at Cabel. "This is too weird," she mouths. Points at the door. Cabel nods and they step out. Closing the door again. "Too weird," Janie says aloud. It's more than she can deal with. "Let's go. Let's just . . . go work out or mess around or get lunch or something. I gotta get this guy out of my head."

12:30 p.m.

They stop at Frank's Bar and Grille and run into half a dozen cops who are on their way out.

"Come back from vacation early just because you missed us?" Jason Baker teases.

Janie likes him. "You wish. Little family emergency brought us home early. It's all fine now," she says lightly.

Cabel and Janie sit up at the counter for a quick lunch. Janie gets a free milkshake for being narc girl.

It's not all bad.

1:41 p.m.

Janie slings her smooth leg over Cabel's hairy one.

Their toes play together quietly while they work in Cabe's basement.

Janie searches WebMD for brain illnesses and injuries and gets nowhere—there are way too many to narrow down.

Cabel Googles "Henry Feingold." "Well," he says. "There's no information on a Henry Feingold in Fieldridge, Michigan. There's a pretty prolific author with that name, but he doesn't appear to be the same guy. Whatever your dad does—er, did—for a living, it's not out there on the Internet. At least not under his real name."

Janie closes the lid of her laptop. Sighs. "This is impossible, trying to figure him out. I wonder why they're not doing anything for him, you know?"

"Maybe he doesn't have insurance," Cabel says in a low voice. "Not trying to judge him by the way he looks, but he's no corporate exec, obviously."

"That's probably it." Janie closes her eyes. Rests her

head on Cabel's shoulder. Thinks about the two people that are related to her. Her mother—alcoholic-thin, greasy, stringy hair, old and brittle-looking in her mid-thirties; her father some sort of weird cross between Rupert from *Survivor* and Hagrid. "How can you even stand to think about what I'll look like in fifteen years when I'm all blind and gnarled, Cabe? Good fucking grief, what a familial circus of deformity."

"Why do you care so much about how you'll look?" He strokes her thigh. "You'll always be beautiful to me." He says it casually, but Janie can hear the strain in his voice.

"Still, they're both such freaks."

Cabel smiles. He sets his laptop on the floor, takes Janie's from her and does the same, and then slowly pushes against her until she's lying on her back. She giggles. He lies on top of her, pressing against her, squeezing her just like she likes. She wraps her arms around his neck, pulling his nose to hers. "I lurve you, circus freak," Cabel says.

It almost hurts to hear him say that.

"I lurve you, too, you big lumpy monster man," Janie says.

That hurts even more to say.

And then they kiss.

Slowly, gently.

Because with the right person, sometimes kissing feels like healing.

Still, something edges to the front of Janie's mind. Wonders if it's worth it—worth going blind, when there's another option.

Besides, what if Cabel won't own up to his fears about being with her?

It's fucking scary, is what it is.

It's like Cabe's the one who's blind.

The kissing slows and Cabel rests his face in crook of Janie's neck, nibbling her flushed skin. "What are you thinking about?"

"Uh . . . besides you?"

"Clever," Cabel says, a grin spreading, his moving lips tickling Janie's neck. He nips at her. "Yes, besides me. If it's possible for you to think about anything else, that is."

"Oh," she says. "If there were anything else, it would probably be how I need to get some cajones and go confront my mother." Absently, she smooths his hair away from his eyes. "Try and figure out what happened with them, and with me, and what we're supposed to do now with hermit dude."

Cabel sits back and nods. And then he hoists himself up with a grunt. Pulls Janie to her feet too. "You want me to come with you?"

"I think it'll be better if I do it alone. But thanks."

"I figured. Call me, 'kay?"

Freakishly, Janie's phone rings as he says it.

"It's Carrie—I gotta take this." Janie blows a kiss to Cabel as she ascends the stairs and she answers it. "Carrie!"

"Yo, bitch, my phone's charged up again. How's the whole family soap opera going today? You okay?"

"It's weird, and it's a mess, but it's okay. Thank you again for taking care of my mother. You're the best."

"No problem. Somebody's gotta clean up the neighborhood, right?"

"Ouch. Jeez, Carrie!" But Janie chuckles anyway.

"Well, you know where to find me if you need me," Carrie says. "Hey?"

"Hey what?"

"I'm engaged."

"What?"

"Stu asked me last night."

"Oh Em Gee what the Ef barbecue!" Janie says. "And you said yes?"

"Obviously, since I just said I was engaged."

"Wow, Carrie. Are you . . . are you sure? Are you happy about it?"

"Yeah. I mean yes, totally! I know Stu's the guy I want to be with."

"But?"

"But I wasn't quite expecting it yet."

Janie, having walked from Cabel's to her own house, walks to Carrie's instead. "Are you home?"

"Yeah."

"Can I come in?"

"Sweet," Carrie says, sounding relieved. "Yeah, come on in. My room, of course."

"Okay, bye." Janie hangs up her phone and lets herself in. She barges into Carrie's room and flops down on the bed. Carrie sits at a little dressing table, working her hair with a straightening wand in front of the mirror.

"So," Janie says. "You got a ring or what?"

Carrie grins and holds out her hand. "It feels weird. It's sort of embarrassing, you know?"

"What did your mom say?"

"She said I better not be pregnant."

Janie snorts. "What the hell is wrong with our parents, anyway? Wait—you're not, are you?"

"Of course not! Sheesh, Janers! I may not have gotten the best grades in school, but I'm not stupid. You know I'm on the Pill. And his Jimmy doesn't get near me without a raincoat, yadamean? Ain't nothin' getting through my little fortress!"

"Okay, good. Sheesh." Janie laughs again. "So . . . but you sounded a little like you're not sure about this."

Carrie sets the straightening wand on her dressing table and sighs. "I want to marry Stu. I do. There's nobody else and he's not pressuring me or anything. But he talked about setting a date, like next summer so I can get in my year of beauty school first but I'm just . . . I don't know. It's such a huge thing. I don't want to screw it up."

Janie remains quiet and lets Carrie get it all out. It feels weird to be normal again, sitting and hanging out with Carrie.

Janie wouldn't mind trading problems with her.

"Anyway, that's my junk of the day. What are you up to?" Carrie smoothes her straightened hair with some gooey, shiny product.

"I gotta go home, try and figure out what the deal is with my mother and this guy Henry. I don't have a clue what's going on. I need to get my mother to talk to me."

Carrie looks at Janie in the mirror shakes her head. "Good luck with that. Talking to your mom is like talking to that Godot guy."

Janie laughs. Loves Carrie. Says, "Maybe I'll just get drunk with her and we'll fight it out, barroom style."

"Heh. Call me if you do that. I'd like to watch."

Janie grins and gives Carrie a quick hug. "Will do."

As Janie walks home, she thinks maybe that's not such a bad idea.

SHE SPEAKS

4:01 p.m.

Janie takes a few deep breaths, filling herself with confidence that's not quite there. But she'll take what she can get. She grabs a can of beer from the fridge stash and pops it open, taking a bitter sip. She hasn't had any alcohol since the night at Durbin's, so this feels a little creepy.

She waits on the couch, hoping her mother will come out on her own.

4:46 p.m.

Still waiting. Beer gone.

Grabs another beer. Turns on the TV and watches *Judge Judy*.

Switches the channel to a game show—judges conjure up too many bad memories.

5:39 p.m.

Where the hell is she? Figures she's got to go after her. Right after she pees.

5:43 p.m.

Janie opens her mother's door, two cans of beer in hand. One as an offering. Or maybe a bribe. But then Janie falls to the floor unceremoniously, dropping the cans, sucked into a dream. She hears a pop and a fizzing sound and knows at least one can broke open.

The noise isn't even enough to rouse Dorothea Hannagan from her drunken stupor. *Damn it*, Janie thinks. *Dreams plus booze equals not cool.*

Janie's head spins as she tries and fails to pull out of the dream.

They are in a line outside a building, Dorothea jiggling a crying baby. Janie knows she is the baby—who else would it be? They move slowly but the building moves too, farther away, making the wait endless. It's a shelter, or maybe a food bank. Janie stands in the road, watching her mother, trying to get her attention. Maybe this time, Janie can help change it. "Look at me," Janie thinks, trying to concentrate. "Look at me."

But Janie's sensibilities are off, not strong enough at the moment, and Dorothea merely glances at Janie and then looks away. She grows more impatient as she waits in line. Finally, Janie pulls her gaze away from her mother and looks to the front of the line, to the building. There are two windows.

Above the windows, a giant sign.

"Babies for Food."

That's what the sign says.

Janie watches people deposit their babies in one window and take a box of food from the other.

With all her might, Janie wants to scream, but she can't. She pulls her strength together and crawls blindly across the floor to the bed, butting her head up against it, flailing her numb arms on top of the mattress, not even sure if she's hitting her mother, trying to wake her. Trying to get out of this nightmare.

Finally, everything goes black.

At the same time, from both yelling mouths:
"What is wrong with you?"

Janie still can't see. She's feeling wet, soaked by the beer can that exploded. Dorothea shoves Janie. "What the hell are you doing?"

Janie pretends she can see. Her eyes are open, after all. "I—I tripped."

"Get outa here, you good for nothing—"

"Stop it!" Janie is half-drunk, confused, and blind. But she's done with this. "Stop talking to me like that! Don't give me that 'good for nothing' bullshit. Without me, you'd be on the street and you know it, so just shut your damn mouth!"

Janie's mother is stunned.

Janie is shocked by her own words.

Thus, the silence.

As the world comes back into view for Janie and she can move once again, she gets unsteadily to her feet and picks up the cans. "What a freaking mess," she mutters. "I'll be right back."

Janie returns with dishcloths and starts wiping it up. "You know, Mother, it wouldn't kill you to help me."

After a minute, Janie's mother eases her way to the floor and helps. "You been drinking?" Dorothea grunts.

"So what? Why should you care?" Janie's still pissed off and a little freaked out by the nightmare. "Why do you hate me so much?"

Janie's mother leans over to reach a wet spot on the floor. When she speaks, her voice is softer. "I don't hate you."

Janie's frustrated. "What's going on? What's the deal

with this Henry guy? I think I deserve to know what happened."

Dorothea looks away. Shrugs. "He's your father."

"Yeah, you mentioned that. What, do I have to ask specific questions here or can you just tell me about him? Sheesh!"

Dorothea frowns. "His name's Henry Feingold. We met in Chicago when I was sixteen. He was a student at U of M, but home for the summer. Working over at Lou Malnati's Pizzeria in Lincolnwood. I worked there too, waitressing."

Janie tries to imagine her mother actually working. "And then what? He got you pregnant and took off? He's an asshole? How did you end up here in Fieldridge?"

"Forget it. I'm not talking about this."

"Come on, Mother. Where does he live?"

"No idea. Around here somewheres. I quit school. Followed him here. We lived together for a while and then he took off and I never saw him again. There. Happy?"

"Did he know you were pregnant?"

"No. None of his business."

"But—but—how did you know he was in the hospital?"

Janie's mother has a vacant look in her eyes, now. "He had one of them legal papers—gave it to the paramedics. He had me down as the person to contact. It says he don't want any heroic measures. That's what the nurse told me."

Janie is silent.

Dorothea continues, softer. "I think maybe I oughta have one of them papers too. So you don't have to keep me hanging on when my liver rots out."

Janie looks away and sighs.

Feels like she's supposed to protest.

But who is she kidding? "Yeah," she says. "Maybe."

Dorothea lies down on the bed again. Turns away. "I mean it. I don't want to talk no more about this. I'm done with it."

After a moment of quiet, Janie gets up, unsteadily walks to the bathroom, throws up a few cans worth of cheap beer, and then some. "Never again," she echoes.

Then she crawls into her room, closes the door, climbs into bed and sleeps.

2:12 a.m.

Janie's running.

And running.

All night long.

She never gets there.

SATURDAY

August 5, 2006, 8:32 a.m.

"Yes," croaks Janie into her cell phone. "What." She's still half-asleep.

"Janie, is everything all right?"

Janie's silent. She should know this voice, but she doesn't.

"Janie? It's Captain. Are you there?"

"Oh!" Janie says. "God, I'm sorry, I—"

"Sorry I woke you. I normally wouldn't call but I heard from Baker that you had a family emergency and you're back in town. I'm calling to ask if everything is all right. And to find out more, if you're willing to tell me. Which you'd better be."

"I—ugh, it's complicated," Janie says. She rolls onto her back. Her mouth feels like it's stuffed with toilet paper. "Everything's fine, though. Well, I mean . . . it's a long story." *Ugh.*

"I have time."

"Can I get back to you? Somebody's buzzing me on the other line."

"I'll hold."

Janie smiles through the dull pain in her head and switches over to the other call.

It's Cabe. "Hey, baby, everything okay? What happened last night?"

"Yeah, let me call you back in a few."

"Done." He hangs up.

Janie switches back to Captain. "I'm back," she says.

"Fine."

"And, uh, I'd rather not go into all the details. So." Janie's feeling bold.

Captain pauses a split second. "Fair enough. You know where to find me, right?"

"Of course. Thank you, sir."

"I'll see you Monday for our meeting if not before. Take care, Janie." Captain hangs up.

Janie flips her phone shut and groans. "What is with everybody calling me at eight-thirty in the freaking morning?"

9:24 a.m.

Showered, fed, brushed. Janie feels a tiny bit better after taking an ibuprofen and drinking three glasses of water. "Never again," she mutters to the mirror. She calls Cabel back. "Sorry it took me so long." Janie explains what happened last night as she walks across the yards, up his driveway, and in to his house.

"Hey," she says, hanging up.

Cabel grins and hangs up too. "Did you get breakfast?"

"Yeah."

"Wanna go for a drive?"

"I—sure. I was actually thinking about going to the hospital."

Cabel nods. "Cool."

"Not that I feel obligated, because I don't."

"Nor should you."

Janie is lost in thought. Going over what her mother said last night, although much of it is fuzzy after all that beer. "I think," she says slowly, "he's probably not a good person."

"What?"

"Just a feeling. Never mind. Let's go."

"Are you sure you want to go if he's a bad person?"

"Yeah. I mean, I want to find out for sure. I just want to know, I guess. If he's bad. Or not."

Cabel shrugs, but he understands. They take off.

9:39 a.m.

At the hospital, Janie moves carefully through the hallways as usual, watching for open doors. She gets caught in a weak dream but only for a few seconds—she barely even has to pause in step. They stand outside Henry's room, Janie's hand tense on the handle.

Static and shockingly bright colors. Again, Janie nearly crumples to her knees, but this time she is more prepared. She steps blindly toward the bed and Cabel helps her safely to the floor as her head pounds with noise. It's more intense than ever.

Just when Janie thinks her eardrums are going to burst, the static dulls and the scene flickers to a woman in the dark once again. It's the same woman as the day before, Janie's certain, though she can't make out any distinguishing features. And then Janie sees that the man is there too. It's Henry, of course. It's his dream. He's in the shadows, sitting on a chair, watching the woman. Henry turns, looks at Janie and blinks. His eyes widen and he sits up straighter in his chair. "Help me!" he pleads.

And then, like a broken filmstrip, the picture cuts out and the static is back, louder than ever, constant screamo in her ears. Janie struggles, head pounding. Tries pulling out of the dream, but she can't focus—the static is messing up her ability to concentrate.

She's flopping around on the floor now. Straining.

Thinks Cabel is there, holding her, but she can't feel anything now.

The bright colors slam into her eyes, into her brain, into her body. The static is like pinpricks in every pore of her skin.

She's trapped.

Trapped in the nightmare of a man who can't wake up.

Janie struggles again, feeling like she's suffocating now. Feeling like if she doesn't get out of this mess, she might die here. Cabel she screams in her head. Get me out of here!

But of course he can't hear her.

She gathers up all her strength and pulls, groaning inwardly with such force that it hurts all the way through. When the nightmare flickers to the picture of the woman again, Janie is just barely able to burst from her confines.

She gasps for breath.

"Janie?" Cabel's voice is soft, urgent.

His finger paints her skin from forehead to cheek, his hand captures the back of her neck, and then he lifts her, carries her to the chair. "Are you okay?"

Janie can't speak. She can't see. Her body is numb. All she can do is nod.

And then, there's a sound from across the room.

It's certainly not Henry.

Janie hears Cabel swear under his breath.

"Good morning," says a man. "I'm Doctor Ming."

Janie sits up as straight as she can in the chair, hoping Cabel's standing in front of her.

"Hi," Cabe says. "We—I—how's he doing today? We just got here."

Dr. Ming doesn't answer immediately and Janie breaks out into a sweat. *Oh, God, he's staring at me.*

"Are you . . . ?"

"We're his kids."

"And is the young woman all right?"

"She's fine. This is really . . ." Cabel sighs and his voice catches. "Ah . . . really an emotional time for us, you know." Janie knows he's stalling for her sake.

"Of course," says the doctor. "Well."

Janie's sight is beginning to return and she sees that Dr. Ming is glancing over the chart. He continues. "It could be any day or he might hang on for a few. It's hard to say."

Janie clears her throat and leans carefully to the side of the chair so she can see past Cabel's bum. "Is he . . . brain-dead?"

"Hm? No, there appears to be some minor brain activity still."

"What's wrong with him, exactly?"

"We don't actually know. Could be a tumor, maybe a

series of strokes. And without surgery, we might not ever know. But he made it clear in his DNR that he didn't want life-saving measures and his next of kin—your mother, I believe?—she refused to sign off on surgery or any procedures." He says this in a pitying voice that makes Janie hate him.

"Well," she says, "does he even have insurance?"

The doctor checks the paperwork again. "Apparently not."

"What are the chances that surgery will help? I mean, could he be normal again?"

Dr. Ming glances at Henry, as if he can determine his chances by looking at him. "I don't know. He might never be able to live on his own. That is, if he even survived the surgery." He looks at the chart again.

Janie nods slowly. That's why. That's why he's just lying here. That, and the DNR. That's why they aren't fixing him—he's too broken. She tries to sound simply curious but it comes out nervous. "So, uh, how much does it cost for him to just be here, waiting to die . . . and stuff?"

The doctor shakes his head. "I don't know—that's really a question for the accounting office." He glances at his watch. Puts the chart back. "Okay, then." He walks briskly out of the room, pulling the door closed behind him.

When Dr. Ming is gone, Janie glares at Cabel. "Don't ever let that happen again! Couldn't you tell I was trapped in the nightmare? I couldn't get out, Cabe. I thought I was going to die."

Cabel's mouth opens, surprised and hurt. "I could tell you were struggling, but if I did break it, how was I supposed to know you wouldn't be mad at me for that? And what did you want me to do, drag you out in the hallway? We're in a freaking hospital, Hannagan. If anybody saw you like that you'd be strapped to a gurney in thirty seconds and we'd be stuck here all day, not to mention the bill for that."

"Better that than sucked into full frontal static-land. No wonder the guy's crazy. I'm half-crazy just spending a few minutes listening to that. Besides," Janie adds coolly, pointing to the private bathroom, "hello."

Cabel rolls his eyes. "I didn't think of it, okay? You know, it's not like I spend every waking moment planning my life around your stupid problems. There's more—"

He slams his lips together.

Janie's jaw drops.

"Oh, crap." He steps toward her, sorry-eyed. And she steps back.

Shakes her head and looks away, fingers to her mouth, eyes filling.

"Don't, Janie. I didn't mean it."

Janie closes her eyes and swallows hard. "No," she says slowly. Doesn't want to say it, but knows it's true. "You're right. I'm sorry." She gives a morose laugh. "It's good for you to say it like it is, you know? Healthy. And shit."

"Come on," he says. "Come 'ere." He steps toward her again and this time she goes to him. He runs his fingers through her hair and holds her to his chest. Kisses her forehead. "I'm sorry too. And that's not like it is. I just . . . it just came out wrong."

"Did it? Are you really saying that you aren't concerned about what's going to happen to me? About how that will affect you?"

"Janie—" Cabel gives her a helpless look.

"Well?"

"Well what? What do you want me to say?"

"I want you to tell the truth. Aren't you worried? Not even a little bit?"

"Janie," he says again. "Don't. Why are you doing this?"

But he doesn't answer the question.

To Janie, that says it all. She closes her eyes. "I think I'm a little stressed out," she whispers after a moment, and then shakes her head. At least now she knows. "Got a lot on my mind."

"Oh, really?" Cabe laughs softly.

"Some great vacation week, huh?"

Cabel snorts. "Yeah. Seems like forever since we were lazing around in the sun."

Janie's quiet, thinking about her mother, her father, and everything else. Cabel, and her own stupid problems, as Cabel calls them. And now, she wonders, *Who's going to pay this hospital bill?* She hopes like hell Henry has money, but by the looks of him, he's homeless. "No insurance," she groans aloud. Bangs her head against Cabel's chest. "Ay yi yi."

"It's not your problem."

Janie sighs deeply. "Why do I feel so responsible for it then?"

Cabel's quiet.

Janie looks up at him. "What?"

"You want me to analyze you?"

She laughs. "Sure."

"I'll probably regret saying anything. But it's like this. You're so used to playing the responsible one with your mother. Now you see this dysfunctional guy, somebody tells you he's your father and boom, your instinct is to be responsible for him, too, since he appears to be even more fucked-up than your mother. God knows we never thought that was possible."

Janie sighs. "I'm just trying to get through it all, you know? Get through the messes one by one, hoping each time it's the last one, and then I look beyond it and realize, crap, there's one more. Just hoping that someday, finally, I'll be free." Janie looks over at Henry and walks over to the side of the bed. "But it never happens," she says. Looks at her father for a long moment.

Thinking.

Thinking.

Maybe it's time to change.

Time to be responsible for just one person.

"Come on," she finally says to Cabel. "I don't think there's anything we can do for him. Let's just go. Wait for them to call my mother when he's . . . when it's over."

"Okay, sweets." Cabel follows Janie out of the room. He nods to Miguel at the desk and Miguel offers a sympathetic smile.

"Now what?" Cabel says, grabbing Janie's hand as they walk out to his car. "Food?"

"I think I'd rather you just drive me home, will you? I need some process time. Better check on my mother, too."

"Ah. Okay." Cabel doesn't sound thrilled. "Tonight?"

"Yeah . . ." Janie says, distracted. "That would be good."

1:15 p.m.

Janie flops onto her bed. Sinks her face into her pillow.

Her fan full blast and blowing on her, window and shade closed to keep the heat out. It's hot in the house, but Janie doesn't care. She's still recuperating from last night. She falls hard into an afternoon sleep. Her dreams are jumbled and random, flitting from a creepy, hairy homeless man chasing her to her mother stumbling around drunk in the front yard naked, to Mr. Durbin threatening to kill her, to a parade with all the people from the Hill lined up along the street, watching. Pointing and laughing at Janie the narc girl.

Then she dreams a horrible dream about Miss Stubin dying, and even though she's already dead, it still hurts. In the dream, Janie cries. When she wakes, her eyes are wet.

So is the rest of her. She's sweating so hard her sheets are damp.

And she feels like somebody beat the crap out of her.

Janie hates naps like that.

4:22 p.m.

She slips on her running shoes, stretches, and heads out the door, water bottle in hand. Thinks maybe this is what she needs. She hasn't worked out all week.

She walks down the driveway, feet crunching the gravel, and eases into a jog. Pounds the tar-patched pavement, her shoes making dents in the black blobs that are made even softer by the sun. Sweat pours down her back, between her breasts. Her legs are tired but she keeps going, waiting for that rush to hit. She runs all the way to Heather Home without realizing where she's going. The rhythmic step, the measured breathing, both slamming bad thoughts and memories through her head, trying to pound them out.

Not really succeeding.

Up the drive and into the cement parking lot she runs and then she stops. Stands in a parking space whose lines look tired from years of wear and lack of paint. Looks up to the sky, above the enormous maples, picturing that night a few summers ago when she sat out here with three of the Heather Home residents for the Fourth of July fireworks. They oohed and ahhed over the display, even though one of them was blind.

Blind, like Janie will be.

Oh, Miss Stubin.

Janie, breathing hard, lowers herself to the hot cement and the tears spill out freely, the pain of being eighteen and in love with a guy who can't talk about what's happening to her, and feeling this huge weight pressing into her chest, smashing her down, holding her back, keeping her from really living like a teenage girl should be living, and she wonders, not for the first time, why all this shit is happening to her. Thinks that she made a horrible mistake, taking the job with Captain and accelerating her own blindness for the benefit of others. Wonders what it would be like if all of it had never happened to her, if she'd never read that damn green notebook, if she'd never ridden that train where it all started when she was eight. If she could actually be in control of her life, just once.

Wonders if she should really do what she's been afraid to do all this time.

Save herself and screw the rest.

"Give me a fucking break!" she shouts up to the fireworks that are no longer there. "What the fuck do I have to do to just be normal? What did I ever do to deserve this crap? Why?" She sobs. "Why?"

Also, not for the first time,
there is no answer.

5:35 p.m.

Janie picks herself up.
Wipes the dirt from her shorts.
Starts jogging home.

6:09 p.m.

She slips into the back door of Cabel's house. Exhausted and empty.

He looks up from the kitchen where's he's fixing a sandwich and blinks at her.

"Hi," she says. Stands there, her tear-stained cheeks streaked with summer road dust and sweat.

Cabel's nose twitches. "Wow. You smell disgusting," he says. "Come with me."

And then he leads her to the bathroom. Turns on the shower. Kneels down to take off her shoes and socks as she sets her glasses on the counter and takes out her ponytail. Helps her out of her sodden clothes. And then he holds the curtain aside for her. "Go on," he says. She steps in.

He watches her, admiring her curves. Reluctantly turns to go.

And then he stops.

Thinks Janie might need some extra pampering.

He slips off his T-shirt and shorts. Boxers, too. And joins her.

6:42 p.m.

"Hey, Cabe?" she says, drying her hair, feeling refreshed. Grinning. Putting all thoughts but one aside for the moment. "You wanna go get Jimmy a raincoat and we'll take care of you?"

Cabel looks at her.

Turns his head and narrows his eyes.

"Who the hell is Jimmy?"

11:21 p.m.

In the cool dark basement, she whispers, "It's not Ralph, is it?"

Cabel's quiet for a moment, as if he's thinking. "You mean like *Forever* Ralph? Uh, no."

"You've read *Forever*?" Janie is incredulous.

"There wasn't much to choose from on the hospital library cart, and *Deenie* was always checked out," Cabel says sarcastically.

"Did you like it?"

Cabel laughs softly. "Um . . . well, it wasn't the wisest thing to read for a fourteen-year-old guy with fresh skin grafts in the general area down there, if you know what I mean."

Janie stifles a sympathetic laugh and buries her face in his T-shirt. Holds him close. Feels him breathing. After a few minutes, she says, "So what, then? Pete? Clyde?"

Cabel rolls over, pretending to sleep.

"It's Fred, isn't it."

"Janie. Stop."

"You named your thing Janie?" She giggles.

Cabel groans deeply. "Go to sleep."

11:41 p.m.

She sleeps. It's delicious.

For a while.

3:03 a.m.

He dreams.

They are in Cabel's house, the two of them, snuggling up together on a couch, playing Halo, eating pizza. Having fun. There is a muffled noise in the background, someone calling out for help from the kitchen, but the two ignore it—they are too busy enjoying each other's company.

The cries for help grow louder.

"Quiet!" Cabel yells. But the calls only grow more intense. He yells again, but nothing changes. Finally he goes into the kitchen. Janie is compelled to follow.

He yells out. "Just shut up about your stupid problems! I can't take it anymore!"

There, lying in a white hospital bed in the middle of the kitchen, is a woman.

She's contorted, crippled.

Blind and emaciated.

Hideous.

It's old Janie.

The young Janie on the couch is gone.

Cabel turns to Janie in the dream. "Help me," he says.

Janie stares. Gives a slight shake of her head, even though she is compelled to try to help him. "I can't."

"Please, Janie. Help me."

She looks at him. Speechless. Shudders, and holds back the tears.

Whispers, "Maybe you should just say good-bye."

Cabel stares at her. And then he turns to the old Janie.

Reaches out with two fingers.

Closes her eyelids.

Janie struggles and pulls out of the dream.

Frozen.

Panting.

The world closing in around her again. She struggles to move. To breathe.

When she is able, Janie stumbles on numb toes across Cabe's basement floor and up the steps, out the door. Across the yards and to her tiny, stifling prison.

Lies on her side, counting her breaths, making herself feel each one, in and out. Staring at the wall.

Wondering how much longer she can hide it all.

SUNDAY

August 6, 2006, 10:10 a.m.

She stares at the wall.

And pulls herself out of bed to face another day.

Janie finds Dorothea in the kitchen, fixing her mid-morning cocktail. It's the first time Janie's seen her since they talked.

"Hey," Janie says.

Janie's mother grunts.

It's like nothing happened.

"Any word on Henry?"

"No."

"You doing okay?"

Janie's mother pauses and gives Janie a bleary look. She fakes a smile. "Just fine."

Janie tries again. "You know my cell phone number is here next to the calendar if you ever need me, right? And Cabel's is here too. He'll do anything for you, like, if I'm not around or something. You know that?"

"He's that hippie guy?"

"Yeah, Ma." Janie rolls her eyes. Cabel got his hair cut months ago.

"Cabel—what kind of name is that?"

Janie ignores her. Wishes she hadn't said anything in the first place.

"You better not get knocked up, alls I can say. A baby ruins your life." Janie's mother shuffles off to her bedroom.

Janie stares at her as she goes. Shakes her head. "Hey, thanks a lot," she calls out. She pulls out her phone and turns it on. There's a text from Cabel.

Didn't hear you leave. Where'd you go? Everything okay?

Janie sighs. Texts back. *Just woke up early. Had some stuff to take care of.*

He replies. *You left your shoes here. Want me to bring them, or?*

Janie debates. *Yeah. Thx.*

11:30 a.m.

He's at the door. "Mind if we go for a ride?"

Janie narrows her eyes. "Where to?"

"You'll see."

Reluctantly, Janie follows him to the car.

Cabel heads out of town and down a road that leads past several cornfields, and then acre after acre of woods. He slows the car down, squinting at the occasional rusty mailbox, scanning the woods.

"What are you doing?" Janie asks.

"Looking for two-three-eight-eighty-eight."

Janie sits up and peers out her window too. She says suspiciously, "Who lives way out here in BFE?"

Cabel squints again and slows as they pass 23766. He glances in his rearview mirror and a moment later, a car zooms by, passing them. "Henry Feingold."

"What? How do you know?"

"I looked in the phone book."

"Hunh. You're smart," Janie says. Unsure. Should she be outraged or eager?

Or just ashamed that she didn't think of it first?

Another mile and Cabel turns into an overgrown two-track gravel drive. Bushes scratch the sides of the car and the track is extremely bumpy. Cabel swears under his breath.

Janie peers out the windshield. The sun beats down between the tree branches, making it a striped ride. She sees something blurry about a quarter-mile away, in a clearing. "Is that a house?"

"Yeah."

After a couple of minutes, Cabel driving agonizingly slow over the bumpy driveway, they come to a stop in front of a small, run-down cabin.

They get out of the car. In the gravel turnaround there's an old, rusty blue station wagon with wood panels. A container of sun tea steeps on the car hood.

Janie takes it all in.

Bushes surround the tiny house. A wayward string of singed roses threatens to overtake a rotting trellis. A few straggling tiger lilies are opened wide, soaking up the sun. All the other flowers are weeds. Outside the front door sits a short stack of cardboard boxes.

Cabel steps carefully through pricker bushes to the dirty window and peers inside, trying to see through the tiny opening between curtains. "Doesn't look like anybody's here."

"You shouldn't do that," Janie says. She's uncomfortable. It's hot and the air buzzes with insects. And they are invading someone's privacy. "This place is creeping me out."

Cabel examines the stack of boxes in front of the door,

looking at the return addresses. He picks one up and shakes it near his ear. Then he sets it back down on the pile and looks around. "Want to break in?" he asks with an evil grin.

"No. That's not cool. We could get arrested!"

"Nah, who's going to know?"

"If Captain ever found out, she'd kick our asses. She's not going to go easy." Janie edges toward the car. "Come on, Cabe. Seriously."

Cabel reluctantly agrees and they get back into the car. "I don't get it. Don't you want to know more? The guy's your father. Aren't you curious?"

Janie looks out the window as Cabel turns the car around. "I'm trying not to be."

"Because he's dying?"

She's lost in thought. "Yeah." Knows that if she doesn't invest in Henry, she can write him off as a problem solved when he dies. He'll just be some guy whose obituary is in the paper. Not her father. "I don't need one more thing to worry about, I guess."

Cabel pulls the car out onto the road again and Janie glances over her shoulder one last time. All she can see are trees.

"I hope his packages don't get all wet next time it rains," she says.

"Does it really matter if they do?"

They ride in silence for a few minutes. And then Cabel asks, "Did you get anything from Henry's nightmare yesterday? I was afraid to ask after our little misunderstanding of doom."

Janie turns in her seat and watches Cabel drive. "It was mostly the same as before. Static. Colors. Woman in the distance and then I saw Henry in the dream too. Always sitting in that same chair. He was watching the woman."

"What was the woman doing?"

"Just standing there in the middle of a dimly lit room—it was like a school gymnasium or something. I couldn't see her face."

"He was just watching her? Sounds creepy."

"Yeah," Janie says. She watches the rows of corn whiz past in a blur. "It didn't really feel creepy, though. It felt . . . lonely. And then—" Janie stops. Thinks. "Hmm."

"What?"

"He turned and looked at me. Like he was maybe a little bit surprised that I was there. He asked me to help him."

"Other people in dreams have seen you too, right? They talk to you."

"Oh, totally. But . . . I don't know. This felt different. Like . . ." Janie searches her memories, thinking back through the dozens of dreams she'd experienced in her life. "Like in most people's dreams, I'm just there, and they accept that, and they talk to me like I'm a prop. But they don't really connect—they look at me but they don't really *see* me."

Cabel scratches the scruff on his cheek and absent-mindedly runs his fingers through his hair. "I don't get the difference."

Janie sighs. "I guess I don't either. It just felt different."

"Like the first day I saw you at the bus stop and you were the only one who would look at me, and our eyes sort of connected?" Cabel's teasing, sort of. But not really.

"Maybe. But more like when Miss Stubin looked at me when I was in her dream back in the nursing home and asked me a question. Sort of a recognition thing. Like, somehow she just knew I was a dream catcher too."

Cabel glances at Janie and then back at the road. His forehead crinkles and he tilts his head quizzically. "Wait," he says. "Wait a minute." He presses down on the brake and turns to look at Janie again. "Serious?"

Janie looks at Cabel and nods. She's been wondering it.

"Janie. Do you have any reason at all to think this dream thing could be hereditary?" The car slows and comes to a stop in the middle of the country road.

"I don't know," Janie says. She glances over her shoulder nervously. "Cabe, what are you doing?"

"Turning around," he says. He backs into a three-point turn and hits the gas. "This is important stuff. He might have some information on this little curse of yours. And we might not have another chance."

12:03 p.m.

Cabel stands at the front door of Henry's house and pulls his driver's license from his wallet. He works it into the crack of the door next to the handle and begins to move it side to side. He presses his lips together as he works, trying to get to the bolt to move aside so they can break in.

Janie watches him for a moment. Then she reaches out and grabs the door handle. Turns it. The door opens.

Cabel straightens up. "Well. Who doesn't lock their doors these days?"

"Somebody whose brain is exploding, maybe? Somebody who lives out in the middle of nowhere and has nothing good to steal? Somebody who's half-crazy? Maybe he told the paramedics not to lock it because he didn't have his keys." Janie steps into the little house, making room for Cabel to follow. "See?" she says, pointing to a key rack on the wall with one set of keys hanging from it.

It's stuffy inside. Kitchen, living area, and bed are all in the main room. A doorway in the back corner appears to lead to a bathroom. There's a radio on a bookshelf and a small TV on the kitchen counter. Hot air plunges into the room through an open, screened window at the back of the house. A thin yellow curtain flutters. Below the window is a table where an old computer sits. It appears from the coffee mug and bowl that the table serves as both an eating place and as a desk. Under the table is a three-drawer unit that looks like it once belonged to a real desk. A few papers rest on the floor as if they'd been carried there by the breeze.

Flattened cardboard boxes lean against the wall near the back door. The bed is disheveled. A nearly empty glass of water stands on a makeshift bedside table made from a cardboard box.

"Well," Janie says. "There's goes my dream of a magical surprise inheritance. Dude's poorer than us."

"That's not an easy feat," Cabel says, taking it all in. He walks over to the desk. "Unless maybe he owns this property—it could be valuable." Cabel shuffles through a few bills on the desk. "Or . . . not. Here's a canceled check that says 'rent' in the memo line."

"Damn." Janie reluctantly joins Cabel. "This feels weird, Cabe. We shouldn't be doing this."

"You'll never find out anything if you wait until after he's dead—the state will take over and the landlord's going to want a tenant who can actually pay the bills. They'll clean this place out, sell what they can to pay the hospital, and that's that."

"You sure know a lot of random shit." Janie looks around.

"Random, *useful* shit."

"I suppose." She wanders around the little house. On top of the TV there are a variety of over-the-counter pain relievers. The refrigerator is half-stocked. A quart of milk, half a loaf of pumpernickel bread, a container of bologna. One shelf alone is filled with string beans, corn on the cob, tomatoes, and raspberries. Janie glances out the window to the backyard and sees a small garden and, off to the side, wild-looking bushes dotted red.

The cupboards are mostly bare, except for a few nonmatching dishes and glasses. There's a light layer of dust all around, but it's not a dirty house. In the living area, there's an old beat up La-Z-Boy recliner, an end table with a wooden lamp on it, and a large, makeshift shelving unit filled with boxes. Near it is a small bookcase. Janie pictures Henry sitting here in the evening, in the recliner, reading or watching TV in this almost-cozy house. She wonders what sort of life it was.

She walks over to the bookcase and sees worn copies of Shakespeare, Dickens. Kerouac and Hemingway and Steinbeck, too. Some books with odd lettering that looks like Hebrew. Science textbooks. Janie removes one and looks inside. Sees what must be her father's handwriting below a list of names that had been crossed out.

Henry David Feingold
University of Michigan

She squats down and pages through the textbook, reading notes in the margin. Wonders if those are his notes, or if they belonged to someone before him. The binding is broken and some of the pages are loose so Janie closes the book and returns it to the shelf.

Cabel is looking through papers on the desk. "Invoices," he says. "For all sorts of weird things. Baby clothes. Video games. Jewelry. Snow globes, for Chrissakes. Wonder where he keeps it all. Kinda weird, if you ask me."

Janie stands up and walks over to Cabel. Picks up a notebook and opens it. Inside, in neat handwriting, is a list of transactions. No two are alike. Janie puzzles over the notebook and then she goes to the front door. Pulls the packages inside and looks at the return addresses. Matches them up in the notebook.

She flips her hair behind her ear. "I think he must have a little Internet store, Cabe. He buys stuff cheap and sells it in his virtual store for a profit. So he's got a little shipping/receiving department over there." She points to the large shelving unit.

"Maybe he goes to yard sales and buys stuff too."

Janie nods. "Seems weird that he'd go to school for

science and end up doing this. I wonder if he got laid off or something?"

"Considering the state of Michigan's economy and rising unemployment rate lately, that's entirely likely."

Janie grins. "You're such a geek. I love you. I really do."

Cabel's face lights up. "Thank you."

"So . . ." Janie sets the notebook on the table and picks up a well-worn paperback copy of *Catch-22*. Pages through it, losing her train of thought. Sees a torn piece of paper used as a bookmark. Words are scribbled in pencil on the bookmark.

Morton's Fork.

That's what it says.

Janie closes the book and sets it back down on the desk. "Now what?"

"What do you want to do? I don't see any evidence that he's a dream catcher, do you?"

"No. But would you find any evidence of that in my house if you looked?"

Cabel laughs. "Uh, green notebook, the dream notes on your bedside table . . ."

"Bedside table," Janie says, tapping her bottom lip with her forefinger. She walks over to Henry's bed, but there's nothing there. Just the water glass. She even pushes aside the mattress and slips her fingers between it and the box springs, feeling for a diary or journal of some sort. "There's nothing here, Cabe. We should go."

"What about the computer?"

"No—we're not going there. Really. Let's just go. And besides, you saw the guy. He's not all gnarled and blind."

"How do you know he's not blind? You can't tell that."

"Yeah, maybe you're right," Janie says. "But his hands looked fine."

"Well . . . what did Miss Stubin say in the green notebook? Mid-thirties for the hands? He can't be much older than late thirties, forty tops, right? So maybe it just hasn't happened yet."

Janie sighs. Doesn't want to go this deep. Doesn't want to think about the green notebook anymore. She walks to the door and stands there a moment. Bangs her head lightly against it. Then she opens it, goes outside and sits in the sweltering car until Cabel comes.

"Hospital?" he says, hope in his voice, when he turns the car onto the road.

"No." Janie's voice is firm. "We're done with it, Cabe. I don't care if he was the king of dream catchers. He's probably not—he's probably just some guy who would freak out if he knew we were snooping around inside his house. I just don't want to pursue this anymore." She's tired of it all.

Cabe nods. "Okay, okay. Not another word. Promise."

7:07 p.m.

At Cabel's house, they both work out. Janie knows she's got to keep her strength up. They have a meeting with Captain on Monday, which means an assignment looms. For the first time, Janie doesn't feel very excited about it.

"Any idea what Captain will have for us?" Janie asks between presses.

"Never know with her." Cabel breathes in and blows out fiercely as he reaches the end of his arm curl reps. "Hope it's something light and easy."

"Me too," Janie says.

"We'll find out soon enough." Cabel puts his weights on the floor. "In the meantime, I can't seem to stop thinking about Henry. There's something weird about the whole situation."

Janie sets the bar in the cradle and sits up. "Thought you said you were going to let it go," she says. Teases. But the curiosity takes over. "What makes you say that, anyway?"

"Well, you said there was a connection in the dream, like you had with Miss Stubin, right? That's what got my brain going and now I can't stop it. And how odd, just the way he lives. He's a recluse. I mean, he's got that old station wagon parked in the yard, so he obviously drives, but . . ."

Janie looks sharply at Cabel. "Hmm," she says.

"Maybe it's all just a coincidence," he says.

"Probably," she says. "Like you said, he's just a recluse."

But.

10:20 p.m.

"Goodnight, sweets," Cabe murmurs in Janie's ear. They're standing on Cabel's front stoop. Janie's not about to sleep there again. It's too hard. Too hard to keep her secret.

"I love you," she says, soulfully. Means it. Means it so much.

"Love you, too."

Janie goes, arms outstretched and her fingers entwined in Cabel's until they can't reach anymore, and then she reluctantly lets her arm drop and walks slowly across the yards to her street, her house.

Lies awake on her back. And her mind shifts from Cabe to the earlier events of the day. To Henry.

12:39 a.m.

She can't stop thinking about him.

Because, what if?

And how is she supposed to know, unless . . . ?

Janie slips out of bed, puts her clothes on and grabs her phone, house key, and a snack for energy. The bus is empty except for the driver.

Thankfully, he's not asleep.

12:58 a.m.

Janie's flip-flops slap the hospital floor and echo through the otherwise quiet hallways. An orderly with an empty gurney nods to Janie as he exits the elevator. Up on the third floor, Janie pushes through the ICU door without hesitation. It's dimly lit and quiet. Janie fends off the hallway dreams and, before she opens Henry's door, goes over her plan in her mind.

She takes a deep breath and pushes open the door, closing it swiftly behind her as everything around her goes black, and then she's slammed by the colors and the outrageous static once again.

The power of the dream forces Janie to her hands and knees. The attack on her senses makes gravity ten times stronger than normal. She sways inadvertently as if to avoid the giant block walls of burning color that swing toward her in 3-D. Mentally she's trying to hear her own thoughts above the noise, and it's incredibly difficult—it's like she's in a vortex of static.

Janie's hands and feet quickly grow numb. Blindly, she turns to the right and crawls, aiming for the bathroom so that if she has to, she can get inside and close the door. As a flaming yellow block swings toward her, Janie lunges to avoid it and feels her head connect with the hospital room wall. Concentrate! she yells to herself. But the noise is overpowering. All she can do is slide forward on numb stumps, hoping she's even moving at all, and waiting for a flash of something, anything that will explain some of the mystery of Henry.

Janie doesn't know how much time goes by before she can't continue moving.

Before she can no longer press on, unable to fight any longer. Unable to find the bathroom, to break the connection.

It's as if she's fallen through ice, engulfed in frigid water. Numb, both body and mind. Even the noise and the colors are muted.

Things stop mattering.

She can't feel herself flopping around wildly.

Doesn't know she's losing consciousness.

Doesn't care anymore either. She just wants to give up, let the nightmare overtake her, engulf her, fill her brain and body with the endless clamor and sickening dazzle.

And it does.

Soon, everything goes black.

But then.

In Janie's own unconsciousness, the picture of a madman, a hairy, screaming madman that is her own father, slowly appears from the darkness before her.

He reaches toward her, his fingers black and bloody, his eyes deranged, unblinking. Janie is paralyzed. Her father's cold hands reach around her neck, squeezing tight, tighter, until Janie has no breath left. She's unable to move, unable to think. Forced to let her own father kill her. As his grasp tightens further around Janie's neck, Henry's face turns sickly alabaster. He strains harder and begins to shake.

Janie is dying.

She has no fight left in her.

It's over.

Just as she has given up, her father's chalky face turns to glass and shatters into a dozen pieces.

His grip around Janie's neck releases. His body disappears.

Janie falls to the ground, gasping, next to the pieces of her father's exploded face. She looks at them, sucking breath, finally able to move.

Raises herself up.

And there, instead of seeing her father in the glass,

She sees her own horrified, screaming face, reflected back at her.

Static once again.

For a very.

Very.

Long time.

Janie realizes that she might be stuck here. Forever.

2:19 a.m.

And then.

A flicker of life.

A flash of a woman's figure in a dark gymnasium, a portrait of a man on a chair . . .

And a voice.

Distant. But clear. Distinct.

Familiar.

The voice of hope in one person's ever-darkening world.

"Come back," the woman says. Her voice is sweet and young.

She turns to face Janie. Steps into the light.

Standing on strong legs, her eyes clear and bright. Her fingers, not gnarled, but long and lovely. "Janie," she says in earnest. "Janie, my dear, come back."

Janie doesn't know how to come back.
She is exhausted. Gone. Gone from this world and hovering somewhere no other living person could possibly be.

Except for Henry.

Janie's mind is flooded with the new scene, a soft and quiet scene, of a man in a chair, and a woman, now standing in the light imploring Janie to come back. The woman walks over to Henry, stands beside him. Henry turns and looks at Janie. Blinks.
"Help me," he says. "Please, please, Janie. Help me."

Janie is terrified of him. Still, there is nothing she can do but help.
It is her gift.
Her curse.
She is unable to say no.

Compelled, Janie pulls herself to attention, to full awareness, scared to death that the horrible din and burning colors will return at any moment, dreading getting anywhere near this man who turns mad and strangles her. Wishing she could gather the strength to pull herself from this nightmare now, while she has the chance. But she cannot.

Janie struggles silently to her feet in the gymnasium. With effort, she walks toward the two, her footsteps echoing. She has no idea what to do for Henry. Sees nothing that she can do to help. Really only wants to tie him up, or maybe kill him, so he doesn't have the chance to hurt her.

She stops a few feet away from them. Stares at the woman standing there, not quite believing her eyes. "It's you," she says. She feels a rush of relief. Her lip quivers. "Oh, Miss Stubin."

Miss Stubin reaches out and Janie, overwhelmed by seeing her again and incredibly weak from this nightmare, stumbles into her arms. Miss Stubin's grip is strong, full of comfort. It repairs some of Janie's strength. Janie is filled with emotion as she feels the warmth, the love in Miss Stubin's touch. "There, you're all right," Miss Stubin says.

"You," Janie says. "You're . . . I thought I wouldn't be seeing you again."

Miss Stubin smiles. "I have been quite enjoying my time with Earl since I last saw you. It's good to be whole again." She pauses, eyes twinkling. They pick up the dim rays of light coming in through the gymnasium's tiny upper windows. And *then she looks toward the mute Henry, who sits ever still. "I believe I'm here for Henry . . . I think to bring him home, if you know what I mean. Sometimes I don't know myself why I'm summoned to other catchers' dreams."*

Janie's eyes widen. "So, it's true. He really is one."

"Yes, apparently so."

They look at Henry, and then at each other. Silent, pondering. The dream catchers, all together in one place.

"Wow," Janie murmurs. She turns back to Miss Stubin. "Why didn't you tell me about him? You said in the green notebook that there weren't any other living dream catchers."

"I didn't know about him." She smiles. "It appears he needs your help, first, before he can come with me. I'm glad you came."

"It wasn't easy," Janie says. "His dreams are horrible."

"He hasn't many left," Miss Stubin says.

Janie presses her lips together and takes a deep breath. "He's my father. You knew that, right?"

Miss Stubin shakes her head. "I didn't know. So it's hereditary, then. I've often wondered. It's why I didn't have children."

"Did you—?" Janie's suddenly struck by a thought. "You're not related, are you? To us, I mean?"

Miss Stubin smiles warmly. "No, my dear. Wouldn't that be something?"

Janie laughs softly at the craziness of it. "Do you think

that maybe there are others out there, then? Besides me?"

Miss Stubin clasps Janie's hand and squeezes. "Knowing that Henry exists gives me hope that there are more. But dream catchers are nearly impossible to find." She chuckles. "Best thing you can do to find them is to fall asleep in public places, I guess."

Janie nods. She glances at Henry. "How am I supposed to help him?"

Miss Stubin raises an eyebrow. "I don't know, but you know what to do to find out. He's already asked you for help."

"But . . . I don't see . . . and he's not leading me anywhere." Janie looks around the near-vacant gymnasium, looking for clues, trying to figure out what she could possibly do to help Henry. Not wanting to get too close.

Finally, Janie turns to Henry and takes a deep breath, glancing at Miss Stubin briefly for support. "Hey there," she begins. Her voice shakes a little, nervous, scared, not sure what to expect. "How can I help you?"

He stares at her, a blank look on his face. "Help me," he says.

"I—I don't know how, but you can tell me."

"Help me," Henry repeats. "Help me. Help me. Help me. HELP me. HELP ME. HELP ME! HELP ME!!" Henry's voice turns to wild screams and he doesn't stop. Janie backs away, on her guard, but he doesn't come toward her. He reaches to his head and grips it, screaming and ripping chunks of hair from his scalp. His eyes bulge and his body is rigid in agony. "HELP ME!"

His screams don't end. Janie is frozen, shocked, horrified. "I don't know what to do!" she yells, but her voice is drowned out by his. Terrified, she looks for Miss Stubin, who watches intently, a little fearfully.

And then.

Miss Stubin reaches out.

Touches Henry's shoulder.

His screams stutter. Fail. His ragged breaths diminish.

Miss Stubin stares at Henry, concentrating. Focusing. Until he turns to look at her and is quiet.

Janie watches.

"Henry," Miss Stubin says gently. "This is your daughter, Janie."

Henry doesn't react. And then his face contorts.

Immediately, the scene in front of Janie crackles. Chunks of the gymnasium fall away, like pieces of a broken mirror. Bright lights appear in the holes. Janie sees it happening and her heart pounds. She shoots a frantic glance at Miss Stubin, and at her father, desperate to know if he understands, but he is holding his head again.

"I can't stay in this," Janie yells, and she gathers up all her strength, pulling out of the nightmare before the static and blinding colors overtake her again.

112

2:20 a.m.

All is quiet except for the ringing in Janie's ears.

Minutes pass as Janie lies facedown, unmoving, unseeing, on the clammy tile floor of the hospital room. Her head aches. When she tries to move, her muscles won't comply.

2:36 a.m.

Finally, Janie can see, though everything is dim. She grunts and, after a few tries, shoves to her feet, steadying herself against the wall, wiping her mouth. Blood comes away on her hand. She moves her tongue slowly around, noting the cut inside her cheek where she apparently bit down during the nightmare. Feels her neck, her throat, gingerly. Her stomach churns as she swallows blood-thickened saliva. Janie squints at her watch, shocked that so much time has gone by.

And then she turns to look at Henry. Runs her fingers through her tangled hair as she stares at his agonized face, frozen into the same horrible expression as in his dream when he screamed over and over again.

"What's wrong with you?" she says. Her voice is like the static in the nightmare.

She bites her bottom lip and still she watches from a distance, remembering Henry the madman. *He's unconscious. He can't hurt me.*

She doesn't believe it, so she says it aloud, to herself and to him. "You can't hurt me."

That helps a little.

She steps closer.

Next to his bed.

Her finger hovers above his hand and Janie imagines him jumping up, grabbing her with that cold death-grip. Tearing her throat out. Strangling her. Still, slowly, she lowers her hand and lays it on top of Henry's.

He doesn't move.

His hands are warm and rough.

Just like a father's hands should be.

2:43 a.m.

It's too late for the bus.

When she is able, Janie meanders her way through the hospital and down to the street. Slowly limps home in the dead of night.

MONDAY

August 7, 2006, 10:35 a.m.

A dream catcher. Her father. Just like her.

Unbelievable.

Janie slips into her running clothes and makes her way to the bus stop. Takes it to the last stop on the edge of town. And runs the rest of the way.

Things in the country are so much slower than they are in town. Janie's feet slap the pavement as she runs along, the whole world seemingly coming to a stop before her eyes. Row after row of ripe corn begs to be harvested—Janie can see the soft brown tassels go by in a blur as she runs.

Her glasses slip down on her nose from the sweat, and

she is reminded yet again that she needs to take in the sights for as long as she can. It makes her sick to think about losing all of this, so she absorbs it, one step after another, until her mind wanders again.

She hears the buzz of tree frogs and remembers how, when she was little, she used to think that the intense buzz was not an animal, but the sound of electrical wires, bustling with energy. When she learned the noise came from frogs, she didn't believe it.

Still doesn't.

After all, she's never actually seen one.

And as she sucks in stale, humid air, the faint odor of cow manure becomes common. Alongside it is the sickly sweet smell of wildflowers and the searing hint of recent road patching.

Janie's mind is clear and her purpose is sure when she reaches the long, overgrown driveway of Henry's house. She slows to a walk, trying to cool down.

Just as she reaches the clearing, her cell phone buzzes in her pocket. She ignores it, knowing it's probably Cabel. Needs to think. To do this alone. She opens the door and steps inside the house.

That eerie feeling comes over her—the one that makes her shiver and feel a little bit dizzy and sick all at the same time when being somewhere overtly quiet and extremely off-limits. Janie huffs, still winded, and the noise breaks the silence. "Talk to me, Henry, you creepy little strangler," Janie says softly. "Show me how I can help you."

She walks to the kitchen, wipes her sweaty forehead on a kitchen towel and grabs a glass from the cupboard. Turns on the faucet. The water chokes and spurts out, a lovely rust color until it run clears a moment later. Janie lets it run for a minute and then fills the glass. Drinks it, the tepid water not quite raunchy enough to make her gag.

She decides to tackle the computer first. Boots it up and realizes that it's on dial-up. Not surprising for way out here in the country, but still totally annoying. "Talk to me," she mutters again, tapping her fingers impatiently on the table.

First, she looks through his bookmarks. Immediately finds Henry's online store account and logs in, his username and password unprotected, already filled in. Janie peruses the online store, called Dottie's Place. Finds a collection of odd, unrelated items including babies and children's clothing, small electronic equipment, books, and glass figurine collectibles. She clicks on a pair of "gently worn" name-brand overalls and reads the description. Reads the words Henry chooses. Sees his intelligence and marketing ability and business savvy all rolled into the little store.

There are several auctions in progress, plus a few that have ended in the days since Henry became ill.

And then she sees his rating. 99.8% positive.

Janie doesn't recognize the feeling that wells up in her chest.

Makes her eyes water.

All she knows is that Henry Feingold has a near-perfect rating.

She's not about to let that record get tarnished.

Janie freezes the inventory. Assesses the items that were already sold and searches for them on the inventory shelves. Packs the few items up and finds the UPS slips in the drawer. Fills them out. Wonders if she needs to call for pickup, but then finds the link online in Henry's favorites. She schedules a pickup for before five p.m. Sets the boxes outside the door so she doesn't forget.

Back at the computer, Janie inhales Henry's other bookmarked pages. A political message board, a cooking website, several links to marketing professionals, a Jewish holiday website. Gardening sites.

Dreams.

And a link to a Wikipedia page about Morton's Fork.

Janie clicks on that last one.

Reads the page.

Finds out that Morton's Fork is not literally a fork. It's

a term for a dilemma of sorts. In summary: a forced choice between two equally suck-ass things.

Janie reads about it and sees a comparison to a catch-22, and she glances at the book on the table that coined the phrase. She furrows her brow. "Okay, Mister Creepypants," she mutters, back on the computer, typing wildly searching keywords. "What are you all about? What's your big choice?"

And then she stops typing mid-word.

She sinks back into the chair, remembering the last time she read about a catch-22. Just a few months ago, in a green spiral notebook.

Knows, of course.

It's clear what Henry chose, years ago.

He didn't have Miss Stubin to help him. To teach him.

He had no one.

12:50 p.m

The rattling, house-shaking noise of a truck breaks Janie's attention. Through the window she sees it rumbling toward her and her heart races, knowing she shouldn't be here. But when the driver raps on the door and she shouts in a friendly voice, "Hey Henry, you gotta sign for this one! You out back?"

Janie hesitates, and then she opens the door. "Hi."

The delivery woman looks up, machine in hand. Sweat streaks her tan cheeks and she has wet stains under her arms. She wears the company brown shorts and her tan legs are covered in bug bites and bruises. She looks surprised and confused for a moment, but then says, "Hi, uh, are you eighteen? You can sign."

"I . . . yeah."

"Where's Henry? Out garage-saling? Well, obviously not, because there's his car . . . Well, you can tell him I saw a sign for a big rummage sale that the Luther'ns are putting on. Over on Washtenaw, Fridee and Saturdee." She looks uneasy.

"Henry's—he won't be able to make it. He's . . . sick. Not doing well." Janie feels her throat growing tight. "In the hospital, probably not going to make it."

The woman's jaw drops. She grips the door frame. "Oh, my heck. You're not serious. Are you . . . who are you?" She pounds a fist to her hip as if to get a hold of herself. "If I may ask, I mean—it's none of my business but Henry's been my customer for years. We're friends." She turns abruptly and stares at the woods, her fingers now fidgeting at her lips and then shoving through her mullet.

"I'm Janie. I'm his daughter," Janie says. It sounds weird.

"His daughter? He never told me he had a kid."

"I don't think he knew about me."

The woman sighs. "Well, I'm sorry about it, that's for sure. Will you tell him I wish him well?"

"Sure, I . . . he's in a coma, or something, but I'll still tell him. But—can you tell me a little bit about him? I mean, I just found out he's my dad when he got taken to the hospital, so I don't know anything. . . ." Janie swallows hard. "You want some water?"

"Naw, thanks. I got plenty in the truck." Still in a state of shock at the news, she swipes mindlessly at a mosquito. "Henry Feingold is a good guy. He don't bother anybody. He might look a little strange but he has a heart of gold. He just does his business and lives here, all alone, but he says he prefers it. He studies a lot on the computer, researching for his business and some other stuff—I think he took an online course once. Not quite sure what, but he's usually always got something interesting to talk about.

"Did he say he was feeling sick at all last week?"

"Nothing more'n his usual headaches. He'd get migraines sometimes. Never got 'em checked out, though I told him he should. Said he didn't have insurance."

"So he's had headaches for a while?"

"On and off. Is that what . . . ?" The UPS woman nods in place of saying the words.

"Yeah. Something in his brain, maybe a tumor. They don't know much, I guess."

The UPS woman looks down at the dirt. "Well. I'm real sorry. You take care. I'm . . . yeah. Heck. I'm real sorry." She picks up the packages that Janie prepared for shipping.

"Thanks," Janie says.

"If something happens, you know—if you could maybe leave me a note on the door? I come by a lot, sometimes twice a day if there's an afternoon pickup. I'd sure appreciate it. Name's Cathy with a C."

Janie nods. "I'll try. Hey, Cathy?"

"Yeah?"

Janie fidgets. "He's not, like, blind or anything. Is he?"

Cathy gives Janie a quizzical look. "No," she says. "He doesn't even wear glasses."

1:15 p.m.

Janie sits in the old La-Z-Boy, thinking it all through. Isolation.

He lives here, he's in his late thirties, he's not blind or crippled.

"Oh, jeez," Janie says. She lets her head fall back in the chair. "What the hell am I doing? It makes perfect sense. I'm such an idiot."

Her phone won't stop buzzing.

"Hey," she says.

"Hey," Cabe says, sounding miffed. "You got something going on or what?"

"I just needed to get away," Janie says. "Why, what's so important that I can't be gone for three hours without somebody chasing me down?" Her tone is sharper than she intends. But Janie was really beginning to enjoy the quiet.

Cabel doesn't speak for a moment, and Janie cringes. "Sorry," she says. "That didn't come out right."

"Okay, well," he says. But his voice is still bristly. "I was calling to see what time you wanted me to pick you up for that meeting we have with Captain. At two."

Janie sits up in the chair. "Oh, crap!" She checks her watch. "Shit, I forgot." She glances around the room to make sure everything's in place and she careens out the door, closing it but not locking it, just as Henry left it. "I'm . . . out for a run. I gotta hightail it home and grab a quick shower. How about one fifty-five?"

"Wow, that's cutting it close. We'll be late. You want me to pick you up from where you are now and get you home faster?"

Janie starts jogging down the driveway, her muscles stiff. "No," she says. "No, I can just meet you at the police station."

"What, you're taking the bus? Captain will be pissed. I'm supposed to drive you. You know that. Come on, Janie." He sounds mad.

Janie's voice jiggles as she runs. She breathes out through pursed lips to avoid the stitch she's already getting in her side. "I know," she says. "I know."

"Where *are* you?"

She slows to a walk. "You know, Cabe, I think . . . just . . . go without me," she says. "Okay? I'm not going."

"What the—? Janie! Come on. Don't do this. I'll pick you up at one fifty-five. It'll be fine."

Janie keeps walking. "No," she says firmly. "I've got some stuff to do. I'll call her to explain. Just go."

"But—" Cabel sighs.

Janie's silent.

"Fine," he says. Hangs up without a good-bye.

Janie flips her phone shut and shoves it back in her pocket. "God," she says. "I don't know if I can do this."

She calls Captain as she walks back toward home.

"Everything okay, Hannagan?"

"Not really, sir," Janie says. Her voice quivers. "I'm not coming in today. I'm sorry."

Silence.

Janie stops walking. "I can't make it to the meeting. I—I think I made my decision."

There is the sound of her chair creaking and a soft sigh on the other end. "Okay. Well." She pauses. "Cabe?"

Janie drops to her haunches on the side of the road and squeezes her eyes shut. Bites her forefinger. Takes in a measured breath to steady her voice. "Not yet," she says. "Soon. I need a couple days to figure out what I do from here."

"Oh, Janie," Captain says.

1:34 p.m.

She stands on the road, not sure where to go now. Home, or back to Henry's. Her head tells her one thing.

But when her stomach growls, she knows the answer.

Doesn't feel right about eating her father's food. So she trudges to the bus stop. Thinking, always thinking.

She knows she's going to have to say good-bye to Cabel.

Forever.

It's just really hard to imagine doing it.

2:31 p.m.

At home, Janie fixes three sandwiches. She eats one, wraps the other two in plastic and stows them in her backpack. Dorothea makes a rare appearance, scrounging around in the refrigerator.

"You want me to make you a sandwich, Ma?" Janie says, not really wanting to. "I've got all the stuff out."

Dorothea dismisses the suggestion with a careless wave and a grunt, and grabs a can of beer instead. She shuffles back to her room.

And then the front door opens.

"Hey, Janers, you home?" It's Carrie.

Janie groans inwardly. She just wants to go back to Henry's house. "Hey, girl. What digs?"

"Nothin'." Carrie saunters into the kitchen and hoists herself up on the counter. Sticks her feet out. She's wearing flip-flops. "Check out my pedi. Aren't you so jel?"

Janie fixes her attention on Carrie's toes. "Totally! Really cute, Carrie." Janie fills up a water bottle at the tap and tosses that in her backpack too.

"You going somewhere?" Carrie looks a little disappointed.

"Yeah," Janie says.

"Cabe's?"

"No." Janie sighs. She'd been forced to lie to Carrie when on assignment during their entire senior year. Doesn't want to now. "Can I trust you to keep a secret?"

"Der."

Janie smiles. "I—I found Henry's house. I'm going to go back out there and try to learn more about him."

"Sweet!" Carrie hops off the counter. "Can I come? I'll drive."

"Uh . . ." Janie says. She wants to be alone, but after trekking out to Henry's once already today, the thought of having a ride there and back is too tempting to say no. "Sure. Can you be ready to go, like, now?"

"I'm always ready to go. I'll go start up the little diva and meet you in the driveway."

2:50 p.m.

"So," Janie says from the passenger seat of the '77 Nova. "No plans with Stu tonight?"

"No." Carrie frowns as she steers the car out of town, following Janie's directions. "Why does *everybody* ask me that whenever they see me without him?"

"Because you're almost always with him?"

"So? I am my own person too. Is that all there is to talk about? Where Stu is?"

Janie sticks her head out the window to catch the breeze on her face and hopes for no dreamers. "Are you guys fighting or something?"

"No," Carrie says.

"Okay. So . . . when does school start for you?"

Carrie brightens. "Right after Labor Day. And it's going to be a blast. Finally! I get to learn about something I actually want to learn about."

"You'll be the best in your class, Carrie. You got mad hair skillz."

"I do, don't I," she says. "Thank you." She turns her eyes from the road for a moment to look at Janie. They glimmer just a little. Maybe they're just watery from the wind. Or not.

Janie smiles, reaches her arm around Carrie's neck and gives her friend a little half-hug. Forgets that Carrie doesn't get a whole lot more encouragement at home than Janie gets.

Carrie pulls Ethel into the bumpy driveway. Ethel protests in squeaks and groans, but Carrie presses onward. "Why the heck does he live all the way out here in freaking . . . freaking Saskatchewan?" Carrie says, giggling.

Janie doesn't bother to point out that the nearest Canadian province is actually Ontario. Nor that they were going south.

Outside of the car, Janie goes immediately to the house as Carrie takes it all in—the overgrown bushes, the tiny, run-down cabin, the door left unlocked. "What, he doesn't lock it?"

"He didn't—at least not the last time he left."

"Well, yeah, I can see that. It's not like he lives in the 'hood, yadamean? Who comes way out here? It'd be a real crapshoot. People out here'd either pull a gun on you or invite you for pot roast."

Carrie yammers on.

Janie ignores.

It's all good.

3:23 p.m.

Janie goes directly to the computer. Carrie bumbles around the kitchen, snacking on raspberries from the refrigerator, but Janie doesn't pay any attention. The computer, still on since she left in such a hurry earlier, takes forever to wake back up, and another forever to get online with the dial-up access.

The dialing noise makes Carrie look over at Janie. "What are you doing on his computer, Janers? That's kinda, like, wrong, isn't it?" Carrie stands in the kitchen, hands on cupboard doors, picking up things and setting them down again.

"Nah," Janie lies. "He's my father. I'm allowed."

Carrie shrugs and moves on to the next cabinet.

Janie puzzles over Henry's shop name. "Hey, Carrie, 'Dottie' is a nickname for 'Dorothea,' isn't it?"

"How would I know?" Carrie says. And then, "Yeah, it sounds like it could be. And a hell of a lot easier to say than that mouthful."

"Yeah," Janie says, and then opens up a new window and Googles it. "Yep, it sure is."

"What?" Carrie yells, now apparently sitting on the kitchen floor. Pans rattle.

"Nothing," Janie says absently. "Just stop—whatever you're doing. You're making me nervous."

"What?" Carrie yells again.

Janie sighs. Her finger hovers over the mouse, deciding. Finally, she drops it, opening Henry's e-mail client.

Really feels like she's snooping, now.

But just can't help it.

Janie smiles, reading his kindly correspondence with his customers, trying to imagine him. Wishes she could have talked to him about all of this.

About his life.

But then a loud crash in the kitchen startles her again and she jumps up, frustrated. "Carrie, what the hell? Seriously, let's just go, okay? Jesus Christ, I can't take you anywhere!" Janie just wants to concentrate, to be able to savor these words. The interruptions are driving her crazy.

Carrie stands on the kitchen counter facing open cupboards, hanging on to a door. She peers over her shoulder looking sheepish as Janie stomps to the kitchen to survey the mess. "I love it when you call me Jesus Christ."

Janie pinches her lips together, still mad, trying not to smile.

The crash wasn't as bad as it sounded.

Mostly just empty tins.

"Look what I found," Carrie says, pulling a shoe box from the shelf. She hops to the floor. "Notes and stuff! Like a box full of memories."

"Stop! This is so not cool." Janie glances nervously out the window, as if the crash of tins in this quiet setting would bring sirens and squealing tires. "We should get out of here, anyway."

"But—" Carrie says. "Dude, you've got to check this stuff out. It's a bunch of clues to your past. The story of your dad. Aren't you totally curious?" She stares at Janie. "Come on, Janers! What kind of detective are you, anyway? You should care about this. There's some little pins and some coins and stuff, and a ring! But there's also letters. . . ."

Janie's eyes flash, but she glances at the shoe box. "No. This is too invasive. It's not . . ." her voice falters.

"Come on, Janers," whispers Carrie, her eyes shining.

Janie leans over and peeks into the box, gently moving a few things around. "No." She straightens abruptly. "And I want you to stop snooping around."

"Ugh! How boring."

"Yeah, well, we're sort of breaking the law here."

"I thought you said—"

"I know, I know. I lied."

"So we could get arrested? Oh, that's just great. You remember I've done that once already, and I'm not interested in ending up in jail again—especially *with* you! Who would bail us out?" Carrie's picking up the tins from the floor and shoving them back in the cupboard. "My parents would absolutely kill me. And so would Stu. Sheesh, Janie."

"I'm sorry—look, it's not like we're going to get caught. Nobody even knows about the guy. Plus, I'm his daughter. That might get us out of a mess. Not that there will be one. . . ." Janie sets the box of memories on the counter and hands the other cupboard items up to Carrie. She's frustrated. Wishes she hadn't brought Carrie here after all. She just wants to have some time alone to sift through things, to concentrate and figure things out.

But time is running out, Janie knows. She's got to figure out how she can help Henry, before he dies. And maybe there's a clue in the box.

Still, Janie's above stealing. Physical items, anyway.

Janie sighs, resigned. "Let's just go, Carrie."

They go.

Janie's fingers linger on the doorknob.

6:00 p.m.

She shuffles her feet up the driveway on Waverly, past the Beemer. "Hey."

Cabel looks up from his seat on an overturned bucket.

He's painting the trim around the front door. He wipes the sweat from his forehead with the sleeve of his T-shirt. "Hey," he says. His voice is cool.

"You haven't called me all afternoon."

"You don't answer when I call, so why should I bother?"

Janie nods, acknowledging that she's a jerk. "So, how was the meeting?"

He just looks at her. Those eyes. The hurt.

She knows what she needs to say. "I'm sorry, Cabe." And she is. So, so sorry.

He stands. "Okay, thank you," he says. "Would you like to tell me what's going on with you lately?"

Janie swallows hard. She rips her fingers through her hair and just looks at him. Tilts her head and presses her lips together to stop them from quivering.

She can't do it.

Can't tell him.

Can't say it. Can't say, *I'm leaving you.*

So she lies.

"It's all this stuff with Henry. And crap with my mother. I can't handle anything more right now. I need some time to get things together." She feels her eyes shift away from his. Wondering. Wondering if he can tell.

He's quiet for a moment, studying her. "All right," he

says, measured. "I get that. Is there anything I can do?" He leans over and sets down his paintbrush. Comes down the steps to her. Reaches toward her face and fixes a lock of her hair that flopped the wrong way.

"I just need some time and—and some space. For a little while. At least until something happens with Henry. Okay?" She tilts her head up. Meets his eyes again. They stand there, face-to-face, each studying the other.

Then, she steps into him. Slips her arms around his waist. His shirt is damp with sweat. "Okay?" she asks again.

He takes her in. Holds her.

Kisses the top of her head, and sighs.

7:48 p.m.

Janie, on the floor, leaning up against her bed. Thinking.

She could just go to bed early.

Tempting.

Not.

8:01 p.m.

Janie eats her sandwich on the bus. Washes it down with water. Walks the two miles from the last bus stop to Henry's house. At least it's not so hot out. And there's still plenty of light.

The sounds of the woods in the evening are louder than during the day. A mosquito flies furiously past her ear. Janie slaps her legs and arms as she walks. She's gnawed by the time she gets there, especially after going down that long, overgrown driveway.

Inside the house, it's decidedly cooler than it's ever been. A decent breeze blows in and because of the trees, the little house has been in the shade for hours.

"Ahh," Janie says when she's inside, the door clicked shut behind her. Peace and quiet. A little house all her own. Janie looks around the place and imagines what it would be like to live here, without fear of anybody's dreams.

Thinks Henry got it all just about right. To run a little Internet store, to have this serenity and nobody bothering you but Cathy the UPS driver . . . and Cathy'd never be sleeping.

She thinks about the money she's been saving for years now, including the five grand from Miss Stubin. She thinks about the scholarship. She'd lose that, if she quit her job. If she isolated herself. But isn't her eyesight worth losing a scholarship for?

Wonders if she could still pull it off on her own if she got a little Internet job.

Or.

What if she just sort of . . . inherited one?

Her skin gets goose bumps.

What if she took over for Henry—in everything?

She looks around, her mind turning. Hell, she practically ran the household already with her useless mother—she knows how to do it. Pay rent, get groceries . . . would anybody even notice, or care, if she just took over this place?

"Why not?" she whispers.

Janie takes a swig of water from her water bottle and just sits there, in the old, beat-up chair, surrounded by the sounds of night, consumed by her thoughts. Suddenly, the whole isolation option in Miss Stubin's green notebook doesn't sound so bad.

"I could totally get used to this," she says softly to— happily!—no one. "Never getting sucked into dreams again." She grins because it feels delicious.

And then she stops.

"Maybe I *could* still see Cabe," she whispers.

She imagines it, spending candlelit dinners together here, or maybe lunch if he can get away from classes. Hanging out a few hours a day . . . making out and being together. Just not during sleeping hours.

It sounds good.

For about five minutes.

And then she thinks about years to come.

There's no way they could ever live together.

There'd be no babies, no family unit, ever. Janie couldn't risk that if she intends to keep her eyesight—having a dreaming child would totally wreck her. Besides, there's no way Janie would pass this dream catcher curse along to anybody.

She's okay with that.

But what does it mean for Cabe?

His future, in a nutshell:

- live elsewhere
- spend a couple hours a day hanging out at the shack
- never marry
- never have children
- never spend a night with the woman he loves

She pictures their time together, what it would be like, day in and day out. Stagnant. Cabel coming over for an obligatory two hours while he juggles school, his house, his job.

Janie knows it would be hell for Cabe.

It would be like visiting hours at Heather Home.

They'd end up talking about crossword puzzles and the weather.

And he'd do it too. He'd stay with her. Even though it would totally wreck his entire life.

That's just the kind of guy he is.

Janie slams her fists down into the La-Z-Boy arms.

Lets her head fall back.

Whispers to the empty room,

"I can't do that."

9:30 p.m.

She looks through all Henry's things. His business records. Notes to himself, grocery lists. Pamphlets on migraines. And online, a plethora of medical websites bookmarked, along with sites that offer ways to deal with pain.

She wonders, if he'd had insurance, and if they'd caught the tumor, or aneurysm, or whatever, early . . . if she'd still have him.

But she wouldn't have met him, that way.

She thinks about him, pulling his hair out, clutching his head. The frozen look of agony on his face. Wonders if he's still in so much pain, lying helpless in the county hospital, now. Thinks about how he begged her for help. She talks to the holistic words on the screen. "I wish I knew how to help you, Henry. I guess . . . I hope you just let go soon, so you can be done with it."

Janie peels her warm, sticky thighs from the plastic kitchen chair seat and looks around the small living room. Imagines him here in this tiny, cozy house away from the noise, the people.

She walks over to the kitchen, where the box that Carrie found still sits on the countertop. Janie's tempted to go through it. Go through the letters that very nearly beckon to her in the light breeze from the open window. But.

Two things.

She doesn't want to read some intimate icky love letter written by her alcoholic, sorry excuse for a mother. And.

She doesn't want to feel sorry for Henry more than she already does.

She's had enough heartache, thanks very much. Enough trouble. Enough of just getting to know someone who understands, right before they go and die.

She'll gladly take over things here. But she's not going to love him. It's too late for that. He's too far gone. And she's got enough heartache coming just around the corner.

Janie takes a deep breath. Shakes her head. Pushes the box back into the cupboard where Carrie found it.

She tidies up the house so it looks just like it did the first time she saw it. Turns off the computer and the lamp and stands there in the dark, listening to the quietness.

Wishing for it—wishing for this kind of peace in her life. And knowing now that she can have it, once Henry dies. This place where she can let down her guard. And live. Where she doesn't have to worry about catching anybody's dream.

Something deep inside her longs for it, more than the longings for anything else. Even Cabe.

Maybe it's a survival technique.

Or maybe, as it's been all along up until she met Cabe, she's really just a loner. Will always be a loner.

It certainly looks that way.

And so she sits down again in the old chair, in the dark, in this sanctuary. Wondering what her life will hold. Wondering how she'll care for her mother, and why she even has to—maybe Dorothea needs to fend for herself from now on. Maybe Janie's just been enabling her all this time.

Living peacefully like this. Keeping her eyesight. She looks down at her fingers. They cast long shadows in the starlight from the open window. Janie wiggles her fingers and their shadows splash in her lap.

She smiles.

And though Captain will be disappointed, and will have to take the scholarship back, she knows Captain would never blame Janie for wanting to try to live a normal life. Janie knows deep down that it will all be okay.

She'll miss seeing Captain and the guys. That's sure.

"Well," she says softly to her hands, flexing her fingers and clasping them together in her lap. "It's decided. Isolation. My choice."

God, it feels good to say it out loud.

Even though it's a lot scary.

There's just one last loose end that Janie's got to tie up before she quits catching dreams altogether. One last puzzle to solve.

It seems fitting to end it this way.

Although it's bound to be the worst one of her entire life.

Janie sucks in a deep breath and lets it escape, making her lips vibrate. She's scared. More scared now to go back to the hospital than she was when she had to go to Durbin's party. More scared than when that strange boy named Cabel first fell asleep in the school library and dreamed of a monster man with knives for fingers.

But.

But.

This is also Janie's last chance to see, and say goodbye, once and for all, to Miss Stubin.

Close the door, as they say. It's fucking painful to think about.

But Janie's going to get through this, figure out how to help Henry, and get it done in one shot, even if it kills her.

Er . . .

Well, hopefully not "kills her." That would ruin everything. Yeah.

HENRY

Still Monday. 10:44 p.m.

It's a long, dark walk to the bus stop. Heat lightning flashes in the sky. Thunder rumbles low and the humidity is thick. No rain, though.

Enough with the mosquitoes already.

Janie snacks on a sandwich and a PowerBar. Stocking up on energy, gearing up for a big night. Wondering if Henry is still alive, even.

11:28 p.m.

The hallways are quiet as usual and the doors are closed. Janie waves to Nurse Miguel and approaches the desk. "Anything new?"

Miguel shakes his head. "The doctor thinks it won't be long now," he says.

Janie nods. "I'm probably going to spend the night . . . just sit with him. Okay?"

"Sure thing, hon," he says. He reaches down behind the counter. "Here's a blanket in case you get cold. You probably know the chair reclines, right?"

Janie doesn't know, but she nods anyway, taking the blanket. "Thank you." She continues down the hallway to Henry's room. Stands there for a moment, taking a few deep breaths. "This is it," she says softly, and then she opens the door. Shuts it quickly behind her as she goes down.

It's different this time.

This time, Janie is flung directly into the nightmare. She's in a familiar spot as before, with Henry screaming out, "Help me! Help me!" again and again. He turns to Janie when she approaches and he continues to scream at her. A stoic Miss Stubin stands near Henry, waits patiently for it to end. Even in her divine state, if that's what it is, she looks weary.

Janie doesn't waste any time. "Henry!" she shouts. "I want to help you! I'm here to help you. But I don't know what to do. Can you show me?"

There's no stopping him.

Janie turns to Miss Stubin. "Why don't you leave?"

"I can't. Not until he's ready to come with me."

Janie groans, realizing now she's not only responsible for her hysterical, nearly dead father's peace, but her beloved Miss Stubin's happiness as well. She puts her hands over her ears. Frustrated, growing frantic because of the yelling. It's unnerving, really. And painful. Her whole body begins to ache.

Henry stands up and walks over to Janie and she steps back, tensing, worried that he'll grab her, strangle her, but he doesn't. "Help me! Help me!" He screams in her ear, making her bones rattle from the intense pitch. She moves and he follows her around. His voice is pleading. He gets on his knees and grasps Janie's hand, tugging at her, crying out. Begging for help.

His voice grows ragged, out of control.

Janie doesn't know what to do. She screams back at him, "Tell me what to do!"

Henry's cries grow even louder.

Miss Stubin waits and watches, her eyes filled with pity. "I don't think he can," she says, but Janie can't hear her.

Janie knows she can't hold on much longer. She can't move. Her physical body is gone from her, and her dream body screams out in its own pain. There's nothing she can do for Henry . . . nothing.

Nothing she can think of.

She turns to Miss Stubin. "Can you try? Like last time?"

Miss Stubin nods. She approaches Henry. When she walks, it looks like she's gliding effortlessly across the floor.

"Henry," she says. She puts her hand on his shoulder.

His screams falter.

Miss Stubin concentrates. Talks to him with her mind. Calms him.

Henry's ragged voice falls away.

Miss Stubin leads him back to his chair and beckons Janie to come.

"There," Miss Stubin says, smiling. "It's really a lot easier this way, Henry."

Henry holds up handfuls of his hair. Shows them to Janie.

Janie nods. "Your head hurts, doesn't it?"

"Yes," he says, cringing, as if talking calmly is difficult for him. "Yes, it hurts."

"I don't know what to do," Janie says. "Do you know how I can help you?"

Henry looks at Janie. He shakes his head. "I just want to die," he says. "Please. Can you help me die?"

"I don't know. I'll . . . I'll try. I can't do anything illegal. You understand?"

He nods.

"Where are we?" Janie asks. "Is this your dream? This dark gymnasium? This is it?"

Henry stands up. "This way." He beckons the other two

to follow. He pushes open the double doors that lead out of the gymnasium. They walk through, into a hallway. There are doors on both sides.

They go into the first room.

It's a synagogue.

A boy convulses in his seat. His father, next to him, reprimands him.

"It's you, the boy, isn't it?" Janie asks.

"Yes."

"A memory?"

"Sort of. That is my dream—my life, over and over."

They go to the next classroom. People are lined up outside it. Henry, Miss Stubin, and Janie squeeze past the line of people and go inside. It's a pizzeria. They walk past tables filled with people eating, laughing, to the kitchen, into the walk-in cooler. There, Henry leans in a corner with a girl. Kissing.

Janie stares. "Who is that?"

Henry looks at Janie. "That's Dottie."

"You mean Dorothea? Dorothea Hannagan?" Janie can't get over it, even though she knew there was probably some kissing involved there somewhere.

"Yes." He sighs. "The one true love of my life."

Janie wants to gag.

Miss Stubin interrupts. "Tell us what happened, Henry. Between you and Janie's mother. Will you?"

He looks tired. And it's cold in there. "There's not much to tell."

"Please, Henry," Janie says. She wants to hear him say it. Wants that validation that she's doing the right thing.

"We worked together in Chicago one summer—she was in high school, I was at U of M. In the fall, I went back to Michigan. She quit school and followed me. We lived together. It was terrible. The dreams. I had to choose—be with her, miserable, or be able to function, alone." He begins to pull at his hair again. "Oh, hell," he says. "It's coming back."

"So you just left her to fend for herself? Did you know she was pregnant?"

"I didn't know." His voice grows louder, as if he's trying to talk above the noises in his head. "Janie, I didn't know. I'm sorry. I sent her money. She wouldn't take it. I'm so sorry." He squats down, head in his hands.

"Are you glad you did it? Glad you isolated yourself?" Janie gets down on the floor by him, anxious to get answers now.

"Help me," he squeals. "Help me!" He grabs her T-shirt. "Please, Janie, Please please help me! Kill me! Please!"

Janie doesn't know what to do. Miss Stubin tries desperately to calm him, but nothing works.

"Are you glad?" Janie shouts. "Are you? Was it the best choice?"

"There is no best. It's Morton's Fork." He falls to the floor with a scream. "Help me! Oh, GOD. HELP ME!"

Janie looks at Miss Stubin in horror and sees the cracks in the scene. Pieces of the dream begin to fall away. She can hear the static in the distance. "Shit," she says. "I can't stay in this."

"Go!" Miss Stubin says.

They clasp hands for a moment. Look into each other's eyes, Janie desperately trying to communicate that she's not coming back.

Not sure if it translates.

But it's time to go, before she gets trapped here again.

Janie concentrates and with all her strength, bursts through the dream barrier.

As Janie lies on the floor, shaking, trying to move, trying to feel her skin, trying to see, all she can think about is the look on Miss Stubin's face and the complete, hopeless desperation of Henry, overcome by his own demons.

Oh.

Miss Stubin.

What an awful way to say good-bye forever.

Slowly, exhausted, Janie pulls herself to the chair next to Henry's bed. Her joints, even her teeth, ache, and she wonders just what happens to her body when she's in a nightmare like that.

But it doesn't matter now.

She is done with them.

Janie wraps herself in the blanket to help stop her body from the uncontrollable shaking. She can barely stand to look at poor Henry's twisted face. Sometime since she'd been here last, Henry pulled himself up into fetal position, hands fisted up by his head, as if to protect himself from the terrible unseen monsters that have taken him hostage. Janie reaches over to him. Touches his hand. Holds it.

She pleads with him. "Please, please just die. Please." She whispers it over and over, begging Henry to let go, begging his invisible captors to let him go. "I don't know how to help you." She buries her face in her hands. "Please, please, please . . ." The words brush the air in rhythmic patterns like willow branches shushing the waves on the shore of Fremont Lake.

But Henry doesn't die.

A half-hour ticks away on the clock. It feels beyond real in the dark, quiet room, like they are in a world cut off from everyone else. Janie snacks on the last sandwich from her backpack, trying to regain some strength, and then she starts talking to her father to help pass the time.

She tells Henry about Dorothea, choosing her words carefully so as not to say anything too negative—she knows Henry doesn't need to hear negative stuff in his condition. Janie talks about herself, too. Tells him things she's never told anybody else, like how lonely she's been.

She tells him that she's not mad at him for not knowing about her. And she talks about her secret dream-catcher life, that she is just like him. That she understands. That he's not crazy—and he's not alone. Everything comes rushing out—dream catching, her job, Miss Stubin, and Janie's plan to just stop all of the dreams and have a nice quiet life like Henry. "I'm doing it too, Henry," she says. "I'm isolating, like you. You probably didn't even know about the real choice, did you? About the blindness and the loss of your hands."

And then Janie tells Henry that she understands why he did what he did to Dottie, even though he loved her so much. She understands that horrible choice. She tells him about Cabe. How much she loves him. How good he is, how patient. How torn she is about what this isolation plan means.

How scared she is of telling him.

Saying good-bye.

It's amazing, having someone who is just like her.

Someone who understands.

Even if he's unable to respond.

Suddenly, Janie feels like she's wasted so much time these last few days, when she could have been here for Henry.

She tells him how hard it's been, discovering all this stuff in the past few days, and she cries a little.

She talks deep into the night.

Talks until she has emptied out her soul.

Henry's face doesn't change. He doesn't move at all.

When Janie is too tired to think or say another word, she drifts off, all curled up in the chair.

All is quiet.

4:51 a.m.

She dreams.

Janie's in her bedroom, sitting up in bed, disoriented. Her tongue feels dry, parched, and she wets her lips. Her tongue leaves a film on her lips—it feels gritty like sand. When Janie reaches up to wipe away the grittiness, her lips give way. Her teeth collapse and tiny pieces break off in her mouth. Crumbling. The sharp, stumpy remains cut her tongue.

Horrified, Janie spits into her hands. Bits and pieces of the crumbled teeth come out. Janie keeps spitting and more and more tooth shards pile up in her hands. Frantically, Janie looks up, unsure what to do. When she moves her eyes, everything is blurry. Filmy. Like she's trying to see in a steamed-up mirror or a waterfall. She dumps her teeth on the bed, forgotten, and wipes at her eyes, trying to clear them, trying to see. But she's blind. "I'm isolating," she cries. "I'm not supposed to go blind! No! I'm not ready!" She claws at her eyes, and then realizes that she has vertical slits—holes in her face—next to each eye. Something pokes out from each.

Janie takes hold of whatever it is and pulls.

Slivers of soap slide out from the slits.

Janie's eyes itch and burn like crazy. She swipes at them and pulls more pieces of soap out, but the pieces seem to reproduce. As she pulls out soap slivers, she runs her tongue over the jagged remains of her teeth, tasting blood. "No!" she cries.

Finally, she pulls out the last of the soap and she can see again. She looks up, relieved.

And there.

Sitting in his chair. Watching Janie with a look of calm on his face.

Henry.

Janie stares at him.

And it dawns on her, after a minute, what she should do.

"Help me. Help me, Henry."

Henry looks surprised. Obediently he stands and approaches Janie.

Janie shows him her handful of teeth. "You can help me change it, you know. Is it okay if I put these back in?"

Henry's eyes speak. They are filled with encouragement. He nods.

Janie smiles a brickle smile. Nods back. Pushes the teeth back into place as if they are Lego pieces. When she is done, she pats the bed and smiles.

Henry sits. "You're just like me," he says.

"Yes."

"I heard you—all the things you told me. I'm sorry."

"I'm glad. Glad you heard, I mean. You don't have to be sorry. You didn't know." She stares at Henry's empty chair.

He turns to her. "I think . . . I think I would have liked to know you."

Janie chokes back a sob.

He takes her hand. "I miss her. Dottie. Is she good to you? A good mother?"

She stares at his hand in hers for a long minute. Not sure what to say about that. Finally she shrugs. Says, "I turned out all right." Looks up at Henry's face.

Smiles a crooked smile through her tears.

6:10 a.m.

The door to Henry's ICU room opens.

It's the first shift nurse, checking vitals. Janie startles awake, sits up and rubs her eyes.

"Don't mind me," the nurse says, checking Henry's pulse. "You look like you could use some more sleep."

Janie smiles and stretches. She glances at Henry, remembering. It was weird, having someone in her dream for the first time.

Then she sucks in a breath, surprised, and hops to her feet to get a better look. "He's—" she says as the nurse turns to go. "He looks different. His face."

The nurse glances at Henry and checks her chart. "Does he?" She smiles, distracted. "Better, I hope."

But Janie's staring at Henry.

His posture has relaxed, his face is no longer strained, his hands are unclenched and resting gently now by his face. He looks peaceful. The agony is gone.

The nurse shrugs and leaves. Janie keeps staring, thrilled to see him looking better, hoping he's no longer experiencing the horrible nightmares. Wonders briefly if there's a chance he could pull out of it.

Knows there's a better chance he'll finally get to die.

6:21 a.m.

Janie, with a plan, goes into Henry's private bathroom and closes the door. She knows she doesn't have much strength, but closing the door is a no-brainer if she gets stuck.

She opens the door and gets sucked in. Slowly. Gently. No static, no bright walls slamming into her.

It's just a dark gymnasium, just one patch of light streaming though the high window.

The hallway's rooms are empty, now.

Miss Stubin, Henry, both gone.

All that remains is Henry's chair.

And on the chair, a note.

My dear Janie,

Much has been demanded of you. And yet, you remain stronger than you think.

Until we meet again,

Martha

P.S. Henry wishes you to consider Morton's Fork.

6:28 a.m.

Janie closes the door on her last dream.

When she is able, she escapes the dream again and trudges through the hallways and outside to the bus stop, takes the bus home, and falls into bed.

TUESDAY

August 8, 2006, 11:13 a.m.

Janie wakes up, sweating like a marathoner. Her cheek is stuck to her pillowcase. Her hair is soaking wet. It's at least 450 degrees in the house.

And she's starving.

STARVING.

She stumbles to the kitchen and stands at the refrigerator, eating whatever she can find. She presses the cold milk jug against her face to cool it before taking a long swig from it. And then she takes an ice cube and runs it all over her neck and arms. "God almighty," she mutters, grabbing a container of leftover spaghetti and meatballs. "I need air!"

Fifteen minutes later, she's in the shower, water temp set to cold. It's almost too cold, but Janie knows the minute she steps out of there, she'll start sweating again, so she keeps the setting on freezing.

When she turns off the water and steps out of the shower, she hears her mother's voice, talking on the phone. Janie freezes and listens for a minute, and then she whips a towel around herself, clutching it at her chest, and opens the bathroom door, her hair dripping all over the floor.

Dorothea, in her nightgown, hangs up the phone. Turns to look at Janie, her face haggard and old-looking. Pale, like the moon. "He's dead," she says simply. Shrugs. "It's about time." Shuffles back to her bedroom, but not before Janie sees Dorothea's lip tremble.

Janie stands in the hallway, dripping, feeling numb. "He's dead," she echoes. It's as if the sound of her voice makes it real. Janie leans back against the hallway wall and slides down until she's sitting on the floor. She tips her head back until it bumps the wall. "My dad is dead."

Still numb.

It's over.

After a few minutes, Janie stands up and marches into her mother's bedroom, not bothering to knock. Dorothea sits weeping on her bed.

"So. What do we need to do?" Janie asks. "I mean, like, funeral stuff."

"I don't know," Dorothea says. "I told them I don't want nothing to do with it. They can just handle it."

"What?" Janie feels like yelling. She moves to call the hospital herself, but then she stops. Turns back to her mother. Says in a way-too-calm voice, "Call them back and tell them that Henry is Jewish. He needs to go to a Jewish funeral home." Janie glances at Dorothea's sparse closet. "Do you even have a single decent dress, Mother? Do you?"

"What do I need a dress for?"

"For the funeral," Janie says firmly.

"I'm not going to that," Dorothea says.

"Oh, yes, you are." Janie's pissed. "You are definitely going to my father's funeral. He loved you, all these years. You might not understand why he left, but I do, and he still loves you!" Janie chokes on her mistake. "He loved you," she says. "Now go call the hospital before they do something else with him. And then call the funeral home—the hospital should be able to recommend one."

Dorothea looks confused, alarmed. "I don't know their numbers."

Janie eyes her coldly. "What are you, fucking eight years old? Look them up." She storms out of the room and slams the door. "God!" she mutters, frustrated, as she stomps down the hallway and enters her room. Still wearing a towel, Janie fishes some clothes from her dresser, tosses them on the bed, and then rakes a wide-toothed comb through her tangled, wet hair.

She hears her mother's door open. A few minutes later, Janie can hear Dorothea stammering on the phone. Janie flops back on the bed, sweating again in the heat.

Damn it.

"Henry," Janie says.

She cries for all the things that could have been.

12:40 p.m.

Janie pulls her suitcase from the closet.

Climbs up into the attic to look for boxes.

She'll have to move her stuff over slowly since she has to take the bus and walk.

Wonders briefly if the keys to Henry's station wagon are hanging somewhere obvious in his little house. And then nixes that plan. That could really look like stealing if she got pulled over. No sense getting killed right before restarting her whole life, either.

She fills her backpack with clothing and grabs the suitcase.

Heads out the door.

1:29 p.m.

Janie sets her things down in the middle of the shack and sits at Henry's desk to write a list of things to do:

- Get through funeral first
- Find rental lease and landlord address for rent payments
- Figure out if utilities are included or if I pay
- Clean house
- Study online store history to find out what sells
- Water garden!! And freeze veggies
- Switch to cable Internet if not too expensive
- Tell Captain the plan
- Tell Cabe

She stops writing and stares at the last two words.

Throws the pen at the wall. Slams her fists on the desk. Shoves the chair back so hard it flips over. Stands in the middle of the room and screams at the ceiling. "My life fucking sucks the meanest one of all! How could you force me to choose? How can you do this to me? Do you hear me? Anybody?"

She falls to her knees, covers her head with her arms, and bends forward into a ball.

Sobs rip through the house, but no one is there to hear her.

There is no comfort here.

3:57 p.m.

Janie stares out the bus window, cheek against the glass, watching Fieldridge go by.

As she walks from the bus stop to her mother's house, she calls him.

"Hey," he says.

And suddenly, Janie can't speak. A garbled sound comes from her throat instead.

"Janie, you okay?" Cabel's voice turns immediately concerned. "Where are you? Do you need help?"

Janie breathes, tries to steady her shaky voice. "I'm okay. I'm home. I'm . . . my . . . Henry died."

It's quiet on the line for a moment. "I'll be right over," he says. "Okay?"

Janie nods into the phone. "Yes, please."

And then Janie calls Carrie. Gets her voice mail. "Hey, Carrie, I just thought I should let you know that Henry died. I'll . . . I'll talk to you later."

4:43 p.m.

Cabel raps on the door. He's carrying a potted plant and a bakery box from the grocery store.

"Hey," he says. "I didn't have time to make you, like,

a casserole or whatever. But I stopped by the store and brought you this. I'm so sorry, Janers."

Janie smiles and her eyes fill up. She takes the box and the plant, sets the plant near the window. "It's really pretty," she says. "Thank you." She opens the box. "Oh, wow—doughnuts." She laughs and goes to him. Hugs him close. "You rock, Cabe."

Cabel shrugs, a little embarrassed. "I figured doughnuts are good comfort food. But I'm going to fix you ladies some dinner, too, so you don't have to mess with it."

Janie shakes her head, puzzled. "What for?"

"That's what you do when somebody dies. You bring them casseroles and KFC and shit. Charlie got all kinds of food when Dad died in the clink, and nobody even liked my dad. I was in the hospital but Charlie snuck me some . . . God, I'm rambling." Cabel shuffles his feet. "I'm just going to shut up now."

Janie hugs him tightly again. "This is really weird."

"Yeah," he says. He strokes her hair. Kisses her forehead. "I'm really sorry about Henry."

"Thanks. I mean, we all knew he was going to die. He's really just a stranger," Janie says. Lies.

"Still," Cabel says. "Anyway, he's your dad. That's gotta feel bad, no matter what."

She shrugs. "I can't . . ." she says. Doesn't want to go there. She's got other immediate things to think about now.

Like how to get her drunk, nightgown-wearing mother to a funeral.

5:59 p.m.

Instead of heating up the house even more by cooking, Cabel picks up dinner. Apparently, the scent of fried chicken and biscuits penetrates the Portal to Sorrow, as Dorothea appears and silently helps herself to the food before retreating once again.

The director from the funeral home calls. Janie first writes things down frantically, then discusses arrangement options with him. She's relieved to hear that Jews have their funerals as soon as possible. That suits her just fine. And with no relatives to contact, they set the service for the next morning at eleven.

After she hangs up, Janie whips through clothes hampers and gets some dirty laundry together for the Laundromat. She shoves the basket at Cabel, and then she remembers that she promised Cathy a note. She scribbles something on a piece of paper and hands it to Cabe, along with a roll of masking tape. "Can you drive out to Henry's and stick this on his front door?"

"No problem," he says. He heads out the door while Janie irons a dress and then wipes the dust off of a pair of ancient, rarely worn flats.

"It's not fair," she mumbles. "It's totally not."

8:10 p.m.

Cabe shows up at the front door with the laundry—fresh, clean, and almost, sort-of folded. "Note's on the door, laundry is finished."

Janie grins and takes the basket. "Thank you. You're wonderful."

Cabel grins. "Laundry's not my strongest area of expertise, but I get by. Can I keep the panties?" He grins and backs out of the house.

"Uh . . . you'll have to ask my mother." Janie laughs.

Cabe cringes. "Oof. Fuck and ugh. Hey, I'll let you get stuff done . . . and give you your space. Call me if you need me. I'll pick you guys up tomorrow for the funeral, if you want."

"Thank you," she says. "Yes, that would be great."

Janie watches him go.

WEDNESDAY

August 9, 2006, 8:46 a.m.

Cabel knocks on the door. "I'm sorry to bug you," he says. "I'm not trying to. I know you need space. But here's a little breakfast so you don't have to mess with it."

Janie bites her bottom lip. Takes the tray. "Thanks."

"Back later." He sprints across the yards back to his house.

Janie knocks firmly on her mother's bedroom door.

"What now?"

"Mother? I've got some breakfast for you," she says through the closed door. "Cabel made it. He's going to be back here at ten thirty to pick us up for the funeral, so you need to be ready."

Silence.

"Mother."

"Just set it on my dresser."

Janie enters. Dorothea Hannagan is sitting on the edge of her bed, rocking back and forth. "Are you okay?"

"Set it there and git outta here."

Janie glances at her watch, sets the plate on the dresser and leaves the room, a sinking feeling in her gut.

She hops into the shower and lets cool water wash over her. It's not as hot outside today. That'll be a relief at the funeral, standing out by the grave site in the sun.

Janie's only been to one other funeral in her life —her grandmother's in Chicago a long time ago. That one was in a church and there were lots of blue-haired strangers there. They had ham buns and sugar cookies and orange drink afterward, she remembers, and Janie ran around the church basement with a bunch of distant cousins until the old people made them stop. That's about all Janie remembers.

Janie chose a grave-site service for Henry. It's harder for people to fall asleep when they're standing around outside.

Even the drunk ones.

9:39 a.m.

She remembers now why she's not fond of dresses.

9:50 a.m.

Janie knocks tentatively on her mother's door.

There's no answer.

"Mother?"

With only forty minutes to go before Cabel picks them up, Janie's getting nervous. "Mother," she says, louder this time. *Why does everything have to be so hard?*

Finally, Janie opens the door. Dorothea is sitting on the bed, a glass of vodka in her hand. Her hair is still greasy. She's still wearing her nightgown. "Mother!"

"I'm not going." Dorothea says. "I can't go." She doubles over, wraps her arm around her stomach like it hurts, still holding the glass. "I'm sick."

"You are not sick, you're drunk. Get your ass into the shower—now."

"I can't go."

"Mother!" Janie's losing it. "God! Why do you have to do this? Why do you have to make everything so fucking hard? I'm turning the shower on and you are getting in it."

Janie stomps to the bathroom and turns on the shower. Stomps back to her mother's room and grabs the drink from Dorothea's hand. Slams it down on the dresser and it splashes all over her hand. Pulls her mother up by the arm. "Come ON! They are not going to delay this funeral for you."

"I can't go!" Dorothea says, trying to sound firm. But her frail body is no match for Janie's strength.

Janie pulls her mother to the bathroom and pushes her into the shower, still wearing her nightgown. Dorothea yells. Janie reaches in and grabs shampoo, washes her mother's hair. It's so greasy that it doesn't lather. Janie takes another handful and tries again.

Dorothea claws at Janie, also now sopping wet in her dress. Janie holds her mother's head back so the water runs over her, rinsing out the shampoo. "You ruin everything," Janie says. "I'm not going to let you ruin this. Now," Janie says as she turns the water off and grabs a towel, "Take off that ridiculous nightgown and dry yourself. I can NOT believe this is happening. I am so done with this." Janie turns abruptly and stalks off, soaking wet, to her own room to find something else suitable to wear.

All Janie can hear is some shuffling around in the bathroom. She runs a brush through her hair and fixes her soggy makeup. And then she goes to Dorothea's bedroom, takes out the dress and undergarments, and carries them to the bathroom. Finds her mother still drying off.

Janie looks at her mother, a bedraggled rat, so thin her bones poke through her skin. Her face is tired, dejected. "Come on, Ma," Janie says softly. "Let's get you dressed."

This time, Dorothea goes quietly, and in the dusty light of Dorothea's bedroom, Janie helps her mother get ready. Brushes her hair, pulls it back into a bun. Flips the light switch and puts some makeup on her. "You have nice cheekbones," Janie says. "You should wear your hair back more often."

Dorothea doesn't respond but her chin tips up a notch. She wets her lips. "I'm going to need the rest of that glass," she says quietly, "if I'm gonna get through this."

Janie looks her mother in the eye, and Dorothea's gaze drops to the floor.

"I ain't proud of that, but it's the truth." Dorothea's lip twitches.

Janie nods. "Okay." She turns as she hears the front door open and Cabel's car running in the driveway. "We'll be right there!" she calls out.

"Take your time, ladies. I'm a few minutes early," Cabe says.

Dorothea drinks the vodka in two swallows and cringes. Breathes a sigh, but it sounds more like a burden than a relief. She takes the bottle of vodka from the table by her bed and fumbles with her purse, pulling out the flask. Filling it, spilling a little, replacing the cap.

Janie doesn't say anything.

Dorothea closes her purse and turns to Janie. Janie helps her with her shoes.

"Ready?" Janie asks. "After you."

Dorothea nods. She walks unsteadily to the hallway.

Cabel smiles as the two approach. He's wearing a dark gray suit and he looks pretty freaking amazing in it. His hair is tamed and still damp, curling up just barely over his collar. "I'm very sorry about your loss, Ms. Hannagan," he says. He offers his arm to her.

Dorothea looks surprised for a minute, but she gathers her wits and takes his arm as he ushers her to the door and outside to the awaiting car. "Thank you," she says with rare dignity.

10:49 a.m.

They arrive at the cemetery early. The grave site is obvious by the pile of dirt, the suspended pine box, and the rabbi and cemetery workers around it. There are several other people standing quietly nearby as well. Cabel pulls the car to the side of the narrow road.

Janie gets out of the car and helps her mother out of the front seat. The three of them walk together as the rabbi comes to greet them.

"Good morning," he says. "I'm Rabbi Ari Greenbaum." He reaches out his hand.

Janie takes it. "I'm Janie Hannagan. This is my mother, Dorothea Hannagan, and my friend, Cabel Strumheller. I am the daughter of the deceased." She's proud she doesn't stutter through it, but she's been practicing in her mind. "Thank you for helping us with this. We . . . none of us is Jewish. Not, really, anyway. I guess." She blushes.

The rabbi smiles warmly, apparently unbothered by the news. He turns and they walk together to the grave site. Rabbi Greenbaum goes over the details of the ceremony and hands each of them a card with Psalm 23 written on it.

Dorothea stares at the words on the card. She looks up at the casket. Glares at it. Her mouth quivers but she remains quiet.

The strangers approach and stand around the grave site—several men and a few women as well. "From my congregation," the rabbi explains. "The men prepared your father's body for burial and sat with him through the night, then acted as pallbearers and carried the coffin here."

Janie looks up, grateful. Thinking this is all so very strange, but sort of beautiful, too. How thoughtful of these people to do this, and to take the time to come to the funeral of a stranger.

They stand near the grave and wait. Even the birds are quiet as they approach the heat of the day.

Janie stares into the hole. Sees a thin tree root, freshly cut, its raw, white end sticking out of the dirt. She pictures the casket at the bottom of the pit, under all that heavy dirt, the roots growing and wrapping around it, seizing it, breaking through the casket, seizing the body. She shakes her head to clear it and looks up at the blue sky instead.

Behind her, Janie hears more cars approaching. She turns to look and sees two black and whites. Sergeants Baker, Cobb, and Rabinowitz get out, dressed in uniform. Behind the cop cars is a black sedan and Captain steps out.

Charlie and Megan Strumheller are right behind, still tan from their week at the lake. And then Ethel pulls up with Carrie and Stu. Janie tears up a little. In the distance, a big, brown UPS truck rumbles up the narrow cemetery road. Janie can't believe it—all these people coming. She looks at Cabe, incredulous. "How did they know?" she whispers. He smiles and shrugs.

It's time.

The rabbi greets the tiny congregation of attendees and speaks for a moment.

And then.

"May he to his resting place in peace," the rabbi says.

Before Janie can think, the cemetery workers lower the casket into the grave and soon everyone is looking down on her father in a box. Next to Janie, Dorothea sniffles loudly and sways. Janie grabs her mother around the shoulders and steadies her as the rabbi begins talking again.

And as Janie absorbs the ebb and flow of the rabbi's words, the musical lilt of the Psalms, a little part of her life suffocates in that pine box in the ground too.

"The Lord is my Shepherd, I shall not want." Janie is startled from her thoughts by the group around her, all reciting aloud. She hurries to find her place on the handout and reads along.

And then the rabbi asks if anybody wants to share a story about Henry.

Janie stares at the grass.

After a moment, Cathy, dressed in her standard UPS browns, clears her throat and steps forward. Janie can feel her mother stiffen.

"Who's that?" Dorothea hisses to Janie.

Janie squeezes her mother's shoulder and says nothing.

"Henry Feingold was my customer, and over the years we became good friends," Cathy says, her voice wavering. "He always had a cup of coffee to offer or a cool drink. And when he found out I like to collect snow globes, he started looking for them when he was buying things for his little Internet shop. He was a really thoughtful man, and I'm going to miss him on my route and . . . I'm grateful to you, Janie, for letting me know that he passed on so I could have a chance to say good-bye. And that's it." Cathy steps back to her spot.

"Thank you. Anyone else?"

Cabel nudges Janie. She pokes him back.

And then, and then.

Dorothea says, "I want to say something."

Janie freaks out inside.

The rabbi nods, and Dorothea takes a few unsteady steps to where she can turn around and face the crowd.

What is she going to say? Janie glances at Cabe, sees his eyes are worried too.

Dorothea's thin voice isn't easy to hear in this wide-open space.

At least, it isn't until she starts yelling.

"Henry was the father of Janie, here. The only man I ever loved. But he left me after I quit school for him, and my parents wouldn't let me back home. He was crazy and a horrible person. He ruined my life, and I'm glad he's dead!" With that, Dorothea fumbles at the zipper of her purse.

"Dear God," Cabe whispers.

The small crowd is completely shocked into silence. Janie rushes over and guides her mother back to the spot where they were standing. She feels her face boiling and red. Sweat drips down her back. She purposely averts her eyes from the guests. Mortified.

It doesn't help that Dorothea manages to get her purse open and makes only a small effort to hide that she's taking a swig from the flask.

Rabbi Greenbaum hastens to speak.

Cabe rests his hand on the small of Janie's back to comfort her. He looks down at the ground and Janie can see the amused look on his face. She feels like stomping on his foot. And pushing her mother into the grave hole. Wonders what sort of sitcom that would turn this scene into.

Janie looks up and catches the rabbi's attention. "May I say something?" she asks.

"Of course," Rabbi Greenbaum says, although he looks uncertain.

Janie stays where she's standing and just looks at the casket. "I've known my father for one week," she says. "I've never seen him move, never looked him in the eye. But in that short time, I found out a lot about him. He kept to himself, didn't bother anybody, just lived the life he was given the best way he knew how.

"He wasn't crazy," she continues.

"Was too," Dorothea mutters.

"He wasn't crazy," Janie repeats, ignoring her mother, "he just had an unusual problem that is really hard to explain to anybody who doesn't understand it." Her voice catches. She looks at her mother. "I think, and I'll always believe, that Henry Feingold was a good person. And I am not at all glad he's dead." Janie's lip quivers. It's like the numbness is suddenly wearing off. "I wish I had him back so I could get to know him." Tears trickle down her face.

When it is clear that Janie has said all that she has to say, the rabbi leads Kaddish, a prayer. Then he smiles and beckons Janie to come around the other side of the grave, guiding her to the pile of dirt. Cabel takes Dorothea by the arm and follows. There are several shovels on the ground. They each pick one up.

Janie takes a heaping shovelful of dirt and holds it over the hole in the ground. A trickle of dirt slips off and hits the casket below. She can hardly bear to turn the shovel. The rabbi murmurs something about returning to dust, and finally she turns the shovel over. The thud of the dirt on the wood hurts her stomach.

Dorothea does the same, her arms shaking, and Cabel does it too, and slowly each member of the small crowd takes a shovelful of dirt and releases it into the hole. They continue to fill it.

And that's when Dorothea loses it.

She falls to her knees, almost as if she's just now realized the truth of it. "Henry!" she cries. Her sobs turn to deep shudders. Janie just stands next to her, unable to help. Unwilling to try to stop it.

Such a mess. Janie can see it now, all the guys at the department talking about Janie's mother the drunk, the one who ruined a funeral, the one who fucked around and had an illegitimate daughter and isn't fit to do much of anything but be an embarrassment. She shakes her head, tears streaming down her cheeks as she gets more dirt.

It doesn't matter anyway.

When they are finished, the mound of fresh earth tamped off, Janie knows she has to face the guests. Cabel gets Dorothea to the car.

Janie lays her shovel on the ground. She straightens again and Captain is there.

Captain embraces Janie. Holds her. "You did well," she says. "I'm so very sorry for your loss."

"Thank you," Janie says, tears flowing fresh again. This isn't the first time Janie's cried on Captain's shoulder. "I'm so embarrassed."

"Don't be." Captain's voice is firm—it's a command. For Janie, it's nice to have somebody else running the show for a moment, at least. A relief. Captain pats Janie's back. "Will you be sitting shivah?"

Janie pulls away to look at her. "I don't think so. What's that, again?"

Captain smiles. "It's a time of mourning. It's usually a week, but whatever you decide."

Janie shakes her head. "We . . . I don't . . . I didn't even know I was half-Jewish until last week. We don't practice or anything."

Captain nods. Takes her hand. "Come by my office

when you're ready. No hurry, okay? I think we need to have a talk."

Janie nods. "Yeah, we do."

Captain squeezes Janie's hand and Janie greets the guys from the department. Janie wants to try to explain, apologize for her mother's behavior, but the guys don't let her get a word in about it. They offer condolences and by the end, they're making Janie laugh. Just like always.

It feels good.

Cathy remains by the grave until the guys have left, and then she approaches Janie. "Thank you for the note."

"He'd be glad to know you came, I think," Janie says.

"I dropped off a couple more boxes. They're sitting outside on his step. You want me to return to sender?"

Janie thinks for a moment. "Nah," she says. "I'll take care of it. I'll probably have something that needs to go out tomorrow, then, so . . ." Janie doesn't want to explain here. She'll have all the time in the world to talk to Cathy next week.

"Just request a pickup like you did last time on the Internet, okay? I'll be sure to get them." Cathy looks at her watch. "I got to get back to work. You take care. I'm real sorry."

"I think you knew him best of anyone, Cathy. I'm sorry too."

"Yeah. Yeah, thanks." Cathy looks down. She turns and walks to her truck.

Charlie and Megan embrace Janie in a group hug. "You gonna be all right, kiddo?" Charlie asks.

"Sure, she is," Megan says. "She's tough as nails. But we're here for you if you need us, right?"

Janie nods gratefully, thanking them.

And then Carrie and Stu are there, offering comfort. Stu's wearing the same shirt and outdated tie that he wore to the senior prom, and it makes Janie smile, remembering. So much has happened since then.

"I can't believe how many people came," Janie says. "Thank you. It means a lot."

Carrie grabs Janie's hand and squeezes it. "Of course we'd come, you idiot."

Janie smiles and squeezes back. "Hey," she says, "where's your ring?" and then she stops, worried.

Carrie grins and grabs Stu's hand with her free one. "No worries. We decided that we weren't quite ready for that, so I gave it back. He's keeping it safe, aren't you, honey?"

"Very," Stu says. "Thing was freaking expensive."

Janie grins. "I'm glad you guys are doing okay. Thanks again for coming, and Carrie—thanks for all you did."

"Most entertaining funeral I've ever been to," Carrie says.

Stu and Carrie wave good-bye and walk through the grass to Ethel, swinging hands. Janie watches them go. "Yeah," she says. "Way to go, Carebear."

Janie goes over to the strangers who remain in a small group, talking quietly. "Thank you very much for all you've done," Janie says.

One speaks for all of them. "No thanks necessary. It's an honor to care for the bodies of the deceased. Our sincerest condolences, my dear."

"I—thanks. Er . . ." Janie blushes. She looks around and spies the rabbi. Goes to say good-bye. Afterward, seeing no one else, Janie makes her way to the car.

"Not one single flower!" Dorothea is saying. "What kind of funeral is that?"

Cabel pats the woman on the hand. "Jews don't believe in cutting down a living thing to honor the dead, Ms. Hannagan. They don't do cut flowers."

Janie closes the door and leans her head back on the seat. It's nicely cool inside. "How d'you know that, Cabe?" she asks. "Ask-a-rabbi-dot-com?"

Cabel lifts his chin slightly and puts the car into drive. "Maybe."

4:15 p.m.

When there's a knock at the screen door, Janie rouses herself from a nap on the couch, her mother safely tucked away in her room. She fluffs her hair and grabs her glasses.

It's Rabinowitz.

"Hi. Come in," Janie says, surprised.

He's carrying a box in one hand and a basket of fruit in the other. He brings them inside and puts them on the kitchen counter. "This is to help sweeten your sorrow," he says.

Janie is overcome. "Thank you." The words seem too small to express what she is feeling.

He smiles and excuses himself. "I'm still on duty but I wanted to drop them off. I'm sorry for your loss, Janie." He waves and ducks out the door.

All of the nice.

All of it.

It only makes it harder.

4:28 p.m.

Lies back down on the couch, full of cake.

Thinks about what happens next.

Knows that soon she'll say good-bye to Cabe forever.

And that?

Despite the benefits,

Will be the hardest thing she's ever done.

6:04 p.m.

She walks up Henry's bumpy driveway, backpack on

her back, carrying a suitcase and a bag of clothes. Two forlorn boxes rest in front of the door. Janie goes inside to deposit her stuff and then pulls the boxes inside.

She rips open the first box and pulls out a baby's snowsuit. Goes over the ancient computer and turns it on. Rifles through the notebook that contains the order log, then opens the file drawer under the table. Repackages the snowsuit and writes the address on the box.

Janie opens the second box. Pulls out a bubble-wrapped package.

A snow globe.

It's not listed as an item that needs to be shipped out.

It's for Cathy, she's sure.

Paris. Janie shakes the globe and watches the golden, glittery snow swirling about the gray plastic Eiffel Tower and Notre Dame.

How stunningly tacky.

Yet totally full of a certain sort of special.

Janie smiles, wraps it up again and puts it back in the box. Writes on the box with a black marker:

TO CATHY, ONE LAST GIFT.

FROM HENRY.

Janie finishes her father's business and then she searches, and finds, the ancient rental agreement. Discovers that

Henry's been month-to-month since 1987, just mailing in a check faithfully so it arrives by the first of each month. It'll be easy continuing on from here.

Oh, she'll let the landlord know Henry passed on. But she'll make it very tempting for the landlord to accept Janie as the new tenant. She can even pay the first year in advance if she has to.

She shuts down the computer.

Pulls the sheets off the bed and puts them in the little old washing machine. Decides she's going to clean up the place and sleep here tonight.

Here, in her new home.

It's such a freaking huge relief.

MEMORIES

8:43 p.m. Still the funeral day.

The first evening in her new place. Isolation, day one.

Laundry done, house dusted, sandwich eaten, grocery list made, Janie sits on her new bed with Henry's shoe box full of memories.

Inside:

- fourteen letters from Dottie
- five unopened letters to Dottie from Henry, marked "Return to Sender"
- a small, tarnished medal from a high school cross-country team
- a class ring
- two envelopes containing photographs

- a loonie and a silver dollar
- nine paper clips
- an old driver's license
- and a folded piece of paper

Gingerly, Janie takes the photographs out of the envelopes and looks through them. Snapshots of Dorothea—tons of them. Photos of the two of them, laughing. Having fun. Kissing and lying together on the beach, blissful smiles on their faces. On the big gray rocks by Lake Michigan, a sign in the background that says "Navy Pier." They look good together. Dorothea is pretty, especially when she smiles. Unbelievable.

Janie also recognizes the living room in the pictures. Henry with his feet propped up on the same coffee table, the same old curtains on the windows, Dorothea stretched out on the same old crappy couch, although it all looks nearly new in the photos. Everything's the same. Janie looks again at the photos of the happy couple.

Well, maybe not everything is the same.

Janie puts the photos in chronological order according to the red digital time stamp marked on the corner of each picture, and she imagines the courtship. The whirlwind summer of 1986 where they worked together at Lou's in Chicago, then there's a break from photos in the fall—that must have been the time they were separated, Dottie in high school and Henry at U of M. Janie peeks at the letters in the shoe box from Dorothea and sees the mail stamps on each opened envelope—all were marked from August 27 through October of that year. *Fourteen handwritten letters in two months*, Janie thinks. That's love.

The second group of photos begin in mid-November of 1986 and the last photo is stamped April 1, 1987. April Fool's Day. Go figure. Janie does the math backward from her birthday, January 9, 1988. *That's about right*, she thinks. Nine months before would have been April 9, 1987. Not much time went by after the last photo before they made a baby, and then it was splitsville.

She fingers the letters, extremely curious. Over-whelmingly curious. Dead freaking curious. She even picks up the first one and runs her index finger along the fold of the letter inside the envelope. But then she puts it down.

It's like the letters are sacred or something.

That, and eww. There's probably something gross written inside. It would be almost as bad as getting sucked into her mother's sex dream. Ick and yuck. Blurgh. Once you read something, you can't erase it from your brain.

Janie puts the letters and the photographs back into the box. She picks up the loonie and wonders how long it's been since her father visited Canada. Smiling, she sets the loonie back down next to the silver dollar and picks up the cross-country medal. She turns it over in her fingers, holding it close to her face and squinting so she can see all the little nooks and crevasses. "I'm a runner too," she says softly. "Just a different kind. The road kind." She holds the medal close and then she pins it on her backpack.

Next, Janie looks at the driver's license. It was his first one, expired long ago. His photo is hilarious and his signature is a boyish version of the one that Janie has seen around the house.

And then Janie picks up the class ring. *1985* is engraved on one side, and *LHS* is on the other. There's a tiny engraving of a runner below the letters. The ring is gold with a ruby stone and it's beautiful. Janie imagines it on Henry's finger, and then she goes back to the photographs and spies it there, on his right hand. Janie slips it on her own finger. It's way too big. But it fits her thumb. She takes it off and puts it back in the box.

Then picks it up again.

Puts it on her thumb.

Likes how it feels there.

11:10 p.m.

After going through everything but the letters once more, Janie finds the folded-up piece of paper with words printed on it. Opens it.

MORTON'S FORK

1889, in ref. to John Morton (c.1420–1500), archbishop of Canterbury, who levied forced loans under Henry VII by arguing the obviously rich could afford to pay and the obviously poor were obviously living frugally and thus had savings and could pay too.

Source: American Psychological Association (APA):

morton\'s fork. (n.d.). Online Etymology Dictionary. Retrieved from Dictionary.com website: http://dictionary.reference.com/browse/morton\'s fork

Janie reads it again. Remembers the bookmark in the book, and the one online. Remembers what the note from Miss Stubin said, about Henry wanting Janie to consider Morton's Fork.

"Yeah, I get it already, Henry. You had a choice. I know." She has considered it—about a million times. She's known it since before she even knew Henry existed. Poor Henry didn't have Miss Stubin's green notebook. Didn't even know the real choice. "I'm way ahead of you, man," she says.

Janie knows which choice sounds like the better one to her. Or she wouldn't be here.

She crumples up the paper and tosses it in the trash can.

She gives a last glance at the letters. And lets them be.

Turns out the light.

Tosses and turns, knowing that tomorrow, she's got a lot of hard explaining to do.

6:11 a.m.

She dreams.

Henry stands on a giant rock in the middle of rapids at the top of waterfall.

His hair turns into a hive of hornets. They buzz around angrily.

If he falls in, the hornets might go away, but he'll die falling down the waterfall.

If he stays on the rock, he'll be stung to death.

Janie watches him. On one bank stands Death, his long black cloak unmoving in the breeze. On the other bank is old Martha Stubin in her wheelchair. Blind, gnarled.

Henry flattens himself on the rock and tries to wash the hornets out of his hair. That only makes them furious. They begin to sting him, and he cries out, slapping at them, futile to stop them. Finally, he falls off the rock and soars over the waterfall. Plunging to his death.

Janie snaps awake and sits up with a gasp, disoriented.

Sits there, sinking back into the pillow, trying to get her heart rate back down to normal.

Thinking.

Hard.

Harder.

And then she pads over to the computer and waits in the cool dawn for it to boot up and connect to the Internet.

Looks up Morton's Fork again. *Why won't Morton's Fork just go away? Why do I keep running into this stupid concept? I know, already. Seriously. I. Get. It. I get it more than Henry ever got it.*

She finds it. Paraphrases under her breath. "A totally suck-ass choice between two equally terrible outcomes. Okay, okay. Right? I KNOW this."

She thinks about it more, in case she's missing something.

Thinks about Henry.

Henry's Morton's Fork was obvious. He chose isolation over the torture and the unpredictable nature of being sucked into dreams. That was his choice. That's what he knew.

Equally terrible.

Yes, Janie could argue that his options were equally terrible. It's a crapshoot. He could have gone either way.

She thinks of Martha Stubin. About how, when she was young, her Morton's Fork was exactly the same as Henry's, and she'd chosen the other path. She didn't know, at the time of her choice, what would happen to her. But then, she became blind and crippled.

Which adds a factor. And it makes Janie's Morton's Fork different.

Janie has the most information of all of them.

Still, this is not news. She's had all this information since the green notebook.

Equally terrible.

The term niggles at Janie's brain and she begins to pace around the little house, the wood floor cool and smooth on her bare feet.

She opens the refrigerator and stares into it, not really seeing anything inside, and thinks about her options.

Argues with herself.

Yes, it's equally terrible. Leaving Cabe and society to go live in a shack, alone? Yeah, that feels pretty terrible. As terrible as becoming blind and crippled? Sure.

Isn't it?

But what if Cabe wasn't a factor?

Isolation. Going off to live alone—hermits do it. Monks do it. People actually choose to do that. To isolate.

No one in his right mind chooses blind and crippled—not after really thinking about it, like Janie did. Martha didn't choose it—it just happened. She didn't know it would happen. No one would ever choose it.

No one.

Unless the only alternative is equally bad.

She's thinking. Thinking about Henry. How he lived. How he died. About how he grew calm, finally. After. Only after he got sucked into Janie's dream.

"There is no best," he'd said during his dream earlier. Holding his head. Pulling his hair out. But he was talking about his version of Morton's Fork. His choice. Janie knows Henry couldn't have known the true choice—he didn't know about Miss Stubin and her blindness, her hands. He still doesn't know, probably, unless she told him. After.

7:03 a.m.

Janie's brain won't let it die.

Because what if?

What if Henry's brain problem actually wasn't a real illness, like a tumor or aneurysm, that normal people have?

What if . . . what if it was a consequence?

The migraines, the pain. Pulling his hair out. As if there was so much pressure.

From not using the ability.

Pressure from not going into other people's dreams.

So much pressure, parts of his brain exploded.

"Noo-o," she says softly.

Sits there, frozen.

In shock.

And then she drops her head. Rests her cheek on the desk.

Groans.

"Shit, Henry," she says softly. She sighs and closes her eyes, and they begin to sting and burn. "You and your Morton's fucking Fork."

THE LAST DAY

Thursday, August 10, 2006, 7:45 a.m.

Janie still sits at Henry's desk. In shock. Denial.

But deep down, she knows it's true. It has to be. It all makes sense.

Can't believe it all comes down to a totally different choice than what she—and Miss Stubin—had thought all this time.

Not between isolation and being blind and gnarled.

But between being blind and gnarled, and isolating until your brain explodes.

"Gaaah!" Janie shouts. That's one great thing about this little house out in the middle of nowhere. She can shout and nobody calls the police.

She slumps back in the desk chair. Then slowly gets up.

Falls on the bed and just lies there, staring at the wall.

"Now what?" she whispers.

No one answers.

9:39 a.m.

She gets up. Looks around the little shack. Shakes her head.

Sorry.

So very sorry.

And now, looking at a fresh set of equally suck-ass options, a true Morton's Fork, she realizes that she has a new choice to make.

She sits cross-legged on the bed, pen and paper in hand, and lays it all out. Pros and cons. Benefits and detriments. Suck versus suck.

Miss Stubin's life, or Henry's?

Which one does Janie want?

"No regrets," Miss Stubin had said in the green notebook. But she didn't know the truth.

"There is no best," Henry had said in the dream. He didn't know either.

Janie, alone in the world, is the only one who knows the real choice.

10:11 a.m.

She calls Captain.

"Komisky. Hey, Janie, how you doing?"

"Hi, Captain—okay, I guess. You have time to talk today?"

"One sec." Janie hears Captain's fingernails clicking on her computer keyboard. "How's noon? I'll grab takeout, we can have lunch in my office. Sound good?"

"Sounds great," Janie says. She hangs up.

Feels the butterflies in her belly.

And then.

She shakes her head and starts packing.

Packing up the things that she brought over here, smashing them into her suitcase to make it all fit. Hoping to carry it all in one load.

She's going back home.

If it weren't for Cabe, she'd probably just risk it. Stay isolated. In case she's dead wrong about what really happened to Henry.

But she's pretty sure she's right.

It's a gut thing.

So.

There it is.

Janie grabs a handle shopping bag from under Henry's sink and fills it with all the stuff she couldn't fit in her suitcase. Shakes her head from time to time.

Still can't believe it.

Before she leaves, she calls Henry's landlord to let him know that Henry died. Then, she closes down Henry's online shop for good, schedules a pickup for the last remaining item, and leaves the snow globe gift outside with a sign so Cathy doesn't miss it.

She sets her suitcase down. Closes the door behind her, leaving it unlocked, just as she found it.

Takes a deep breath of country air and holds it in, lets it out slowly.

Glances at the certainly potent sun tea, still resting on the station wagon's hood.

Picks up her suitcase. And sets off.

Crunches down the gravel driveway like a homeless person, carrying all her crap.

Doesn't look back.

When she gets home, she puts her things away in her

room, and from the bag she pulls the shoe box, all the letters untouched. Janie, medal pinned to her backpack and ring on her thumb, carries the box to the kitchen and sets it on the counter next to the lure of Rabinowitz's fruit and cake.

11:56 a.m.

Janie greets the guys as she makes her way through the department to Captain's office. She stops at Rabinowitz's desk to thank him again for the sweets, but he's not there. Janie smiles and scribbles a note on a piece of scratch paper instead.

Then she knocks on Captain's door.

"Come!"

Janie enters. The smell of Chinese food makes her stomach growl. Captain is setting out paper plates and plastic forks. She opens up the food containers and smiles warmly. "How are you?"

Janie closes the door and sits. "Oh, you know," she says lightly. "Crazy as usual." She takes the napkins and peels one off the small pile, setting it next to Captain's plate.

"Help yourself," Captain says. They dish out food.

It feels awkward, the silence, just the two of them. Eating. Janie fingers the new ring on her thumb and accidentally dribbles brown sauce from chicken cashew nuts on her white tank top. Tries desperately to clean it with her napkin before it sets.

Captain reaches into her drawer—the drawer that seems to have everything anyone could possibly need—and pulls out an individual packet of Shout Wipes. Tosses it to Janie.

Janie grins and rips it open. "You have absolutely everything in that drawer. Snacks, Steri-Strips, food stain wipes, plasticware . . . what else?"

"Anything and everything a person needs in order to live for several days," Captain says. "Sewing kit for button emergencies, hair clips, toiletries, screwdriver set, SwissChamp Army Knife and no, you may not borrow it, it's the super-expensive one. Let's see, dog whistle, dog treats, police whistle, anti-venom, EpiPen, water bottles . . . and the traditional mess of rubber bands, paper clips, and outdated postage stamps. A few pennies."

Janie laughs. Relaxes. "That's amazing." Takes a bite.

"I was a boy scout." Captain's serious face never wavers.

Janie snorts, and then wonders if Captain wasn't joking. One never knows with her.

"So," Captain says. "We have a lot of catching up to do." She adds cream to her coffee. "My brilliant assessment is that your little family emergency last week had something to do with your father dying. True?"

"True," Janie says.

"Why in hell did you not tell me what was up before?"

Janie looks up sharply. "I—"

"We are family here, Hannagan. I am your family, you are my family, everybody here is a member of this family. You don't dis your family. You tell me when something big like this is happening, you hear me?"

Janie clears her throat. "I didn't want to bother you. It's not like I even knew him. Well, not really. He was unconscious the whole time."

Captain's sigh comes out like a warning blast from a steam engine. "Stop that."

"Yes, sir."

"Thank God Strumheller had sense enough to tell me about the funeral, or you would have been toast."

"Yes, sir." Janie's losing her appetite. "I'm sorry."

"Good. Now, your father. Let's talk about him. He was a dream catcher too?"

Janie's jaw drops. "How did you know?"

"You said so in your testimonial. Between the lines. You said he had issues that people wouldn't understand, but you understood, or some such thing. Normal folk wouldn't have guessed what you really meant."

Janie nods. "I didn't intend to say that—it just came out. But yeah, he was an isolated dream catcher."

"Ahh, isolated. Like what you're considering. Well,

no wonder we didn't know about him," Captain says. "How did you find out?"

"I went into his dreams."

"Oh?"

"Uh . . . yeah. Found out some interesting stuff."

"I'll bet. And how did you know his UPS driver, Ms. Hannagan? Seems a bit odd that you've never spoken to your father, but from what she said in her testimonial, you apparently had a previous conversation with this lady in brown." Captain takes a bite of her lunch. "What's that on your thumb? Looks like high school bling right out of the eighties. Mm-hmm. Don't answer that."

Janie grins. Her face turns red. "Yes, sir."

"Quite the detective you are, even when you're not on assignment."

"I guess."

"So. Have you made a decision? What we talked about? The isolation thing?"

Janie sets her fork down. "About that," she says, a concerned look on her face. "I, uh . . ."

Captain looks Janie in the eye. Says nothing.

"I was going to. I mean, I made a decision." Janie's having a terrible time saying it.

Captain's gaze doesn't waver.

"And turns out, it's not going to work out after all."

Captain leans forward. "Tell me," she says quietly, but it has an edge to it. "Come on."

Janie is confused. "What?"

"Say it. For Chrissakes, do it. Share something that goes on in that mysterious brain of yours. You don't always have to hold everything in. I'm a good listener. Really."

"What?" Janie says again, still puzzled. "I just—"

Captain nods encouragingly.

"Okay, I just pretty much found out that Martha Stubin had it wrong. My choices are different—either I become like her, or I become like him. My dad. He isolated. And his brain exploded."

Captain raises an eyebrow. "Exploded. Medical term?"

Janie laughs. "Not really."

"What else?" Captain's voice loses the edge.

"Well, so I think I'll just live at home, then. And, I guess, go to school as planned. I mean, it's a toss-up—blind and crippled in my twenties, dead from a brain explosion in my late thirties. What would you choose? I guess, because I have Cabe, I'll choose blind and crippled. If he can deal with it, that is." Janie remembers his dreams.

"Does he know any of this? Any of it at all?"

"Er . . . no."

"You know what I always say, right?"

"Talk to him. Yeah, I know."

"So do it, then!"

"Okay, okay." Janie grins.

"And once things settle down after your terrible week, and you get to feeling good about school, because you will, we'll talk about you and your job. Okay?"

"Okay." Janie sighs. It's such a relief.

They pack up the remains of the lunch.

"Before you go," Captain says, rolling her chair over to the filing cabinet and opening the middle drawer, "here's something—if it's not helpful to you, just toss it. I won't be offended." She pulls an orange photocopied paper from a file, folds it, and hands it to Janie. Stands and walks Janie to the door. "And if you ever want to talk about that, you know where to find me. Family. Don't forget."

"Okay." Janie takes the paper and smiles. "Thanks for lunch. And everything." She stands and heads for the door.

"You're welcome. Now stop bothering me." She smiles and watches Janie go.

"Yesss," Janie says as she runs up the steps to the street level. One hard conversation over. Goes outside and walks to the bus stop. She opens up the orange paper and squints, reading it.

After a moment, she folds it again slowly, thoughtfully, and puts it in her pocket.

1:43 p.m.

She takes the bus to her neighborhood stop. Nobody dreaming this afternoon.

Walks to Cabel's.

He's painting the garage door now.

Janie stands in the grass at the side of the driveway and watches him.

Thinks about all the things that have happened in the past days. The whole journey she's been on. The lows, and the lowers.

She thought she'd have to say good-bye.

Forever.

And now, she doesn't.

It should feel so good.

But there's still the matter of his dreams.

She clears her throat.

Cabel doesn't turn around. "You're quiet," he says. "Wasn't sure how long you were going to stand there."

She bites her lip.

Shoves her hands in her pockets.

He turns. Has paint on his cheek. Eyes soft and crinkly. "What's up? You okay?"

Janie stands there.

Tries to stop the quivering.

He sees it. Sets down his brush.

Goes to her. "Oh, baby," he says. Pulls her close. Holds. "What is it?"

Strokes her hair while she sobs in his shirt.

2:15 p.m.

In the grass, under the shade tree in the backyard. They talk.

About his nightmares

And her future

For a very, very long time.

4:29 p.m.

It's all so complicated.

It always is, with Janie.

It's impossible for Janie to know what will happen, no matter how hard she tries to figure it out. No matter how much Cabe convinces Janie that he had no idea he was having such disturbing dreams, and admits that maybe he is scared. But also that he really is dealing with things—he really is.

No matter how much they both promise to keep talking when shit like this comes up. Because it always will.

There's just no happily ever after in Janie's book.

But they both know there is something. Something good between them.

There is respect.

And there is depth.

Unselfishness.

An understanding between them that surpasses a hell of a lot else.

And there's that love thing.

So they decide. They decide to decide each day what things will come.

No commitments. No big plans. Just life, each day.

Making progress. Cutting the pressure.

There's enough damn pressure everywhere else.

And if it works, it works.

She knows one thing, deep down.

Knows it hard. And good.

He's the only guy she'll ever tell.

IT IS WHAT IT IS

5:25 p.m. Still the last day.

"Hey, can you drive me somewhere tonight?" Her cheeks are flushed. And she has a goddamned hickey. You do the math.

"Sure. Where?"

"Place out on North Maple."

Cabel tilts his head curiously but doesn't ask.

Knows she won't tell him anyway.

Smiles to himself and shakes his head a little as he goes to the stove to make dinner. "God, I freaking love you," he mutters.

6:56 p.m.

Cabel pulls up to the building. Janie peers out the

window and then checks the orange paper. "Yep, this is it." She's nervous. Not sure about this. "Can you just hang out here for about five minutes in case, you know, this isn't cool?"

"Sure, sweets. If I'm gone when you come out, just text me. I'll come right back." He gives Janie a reassuring squeeze on her thigh and kiss on the cheek. "I'll probably just head down to one of the bookstores around here. Maybe drive through campus and take a walk around."

"Okay." Janie takes a deep breath and gets out of the car. "See you." She walks, determined, to the door. Doesn't look back. Doesn't see Cabel pick up the orange paper from the seat where she left it. He reads it. Smiles.

7:01 p.m.

A dozen people mill around the room, getting coffee and chatting. Mostly adults, but a couple of people who look to be about Janie's age. Janie steps into the room, feeling awkward, not sure where to stand. Slowly she backs up to a wall and just looks around, a fake smile on her face, trying not to make eye contact.

"Welcome," says a stocky, middle-aged man as he walks up to Janie. "My name is Luciano." He holds out his hand.

Janie takes it. Shakes it. "Hi," she says.

"Glad you came. Have you been to Al-Anon before?"

"No—this is my first time."

"Don't worry. We all have something in common. Let me get this thing started." Luciano turns to the room and calls out for everyone to grab a seat at the table. Janie makes her way, and a young man offers Janie some coffee. Janie smiles gratefully and accepts, adding her traditional three creams, three sugars.

The small group quiets down and Luciano speaks. "Welcome to Al-Anon. For those who are new here, this is a support group for people who are dealing with the effects of an alcoholic on your life." He looks at the young man across the table. "Carl, would you like to lead today's meeting?"

Janie listens intently to the introduction and testimonial from a woman at the table who talks about her alcoholic, abusive father. After that, Carl leads a discussion about one of the twelve steps.

It feels good to know she's not alone.

And that Dorothea's drinking isn't Janie's fault.

When it is over, Janie takes some literature from the racks. She slips out of the room, texting Cabe that she's ready, and she goes outside into the cool evening. Thinking. Realizing a ton of stuff about her mother. And feeling, for the first time, that part of the stress of her life, part of the responsibility, has been taken away. It feels fabulous, actually.

Wonders why she never thought about doing this before.

8:31 p.m.

They tool around the U of M campus, first by car, then on foot, wandering through the parks and around the various buildings, Cabel pointing out what he knows about where things are and how to get there. It feels weird, and fun, and daunting, like a strange adventure, wandering the campus of such a huge school. Soon, they'll be a part of it all.

They stop for ice cream at Stucchi's and laugh for what feels like the first time in a long time.

When Cabel drops Janie off, she kisses him sweetly, holds him close. "I'm really happy about our agreement," she says.

"Me too." Cabe says. "So . . . tomorrow . . ." He sounds reluctant.

"Yes?"

"I need some junk for school. I suppose, against my better judgment, we should go shopping."

Janie grins. "Sweet," she says. "I'll bring a fork in case it all gets to be too much for you and you need to stab your eyeballs out."

He laughs. "It would be ironic if I went blind before you did, wouldn't it?"

They share a wry smile. A lingering, soulful kiss.

11:05 p.m.

When Cabe pulls out of the driveway, Janie walks slowly to the house and sits down on the step. Just thinks about things, and things, and things.

Like the time Cabel brought her to this step on his skateboard.

And she thinks about Miss Stubin, and how she never actually had a chance to say good-bye. She's glad for the note on the chair.

She thinks about Captain, and her eyes get misty. *Family*, she'd said.

It's good to have family like that.

Janie turns Henry's ring so it catches the glow from the streetlamp. The ruby sparkles. She makes a fist. Presses the ring to her lips. Holds it there. Then lifts it up to the sky. Says, "Hey, Henry . . ." and stops, because her throat hurts too much to go on.

Janie listens to the crickets and tree frogs—or wires—buzzing in their last days of summer, before the sounds of crunchy leaves take over once again.

She thinks about her mother in a different way. A new way, tonight. Plans on going back to another Al-Anon meeting. Might even share her own story sometime. If she feels like it. Or not. No rash decisions. No big commitments. Each day as it comes.

Janie takes a deep breath and feels the briskness of the night filling her lungs. She sits a moment more on the step, and then eases to her feet and peers into the house through the kitchen window, pushing her face against the dusty old screen, wrapping her hands around her glasses to shield against the glare from the streetlights. Streams of soft light from the window cut diagonally across the kitchen.

The box of memories is gone.

So is the cake.

Janie laughs quietly, but inside, she aches a little. For a moment, she left all this trouble behind. And now here she is again, and will be, for a while at least.

It's hard to get excited about that.

But life goes on.

Everything progresses in one direction or another. Relationships, abilities, illnesses, disabilities. Knowledge.

School. A new life where few will know her. Where few will call her narc girl. But where many will dream.

She sighs.

One day at a time. One dream at a time.

Her choice is made. For now. For today.

"This is it," she whispers to the buzzing wires. "This is really it."

The chill of the evening, the preamble to autumn, has arrived, and Janie rubs her bare arms, covered in goose bumps.

It's exhausting to think about it all. Quietly, she goes inside. Locks the door behind her. Slips off her shoes and tosses her backpack on the couch. But before Janie says a last good night tonight, she has just one more task in mind.

She pads on bare feet down the short hallway in the quiet night.

And pauses at the portal to another world.

There's just one more sorrow's dream to change.